Renfrewshire
Council

THE SQUEALER

Who killed Sir James Maddox? Inspector Burnett thinks he knows. He arrests Dick Mason, found standing over the body with a poker in his hand. Though Peter Escott, crime reporter for the *Megaphone*, has other ideas and, with the assistance of Chief Inspector Trimmer, sets out to prove that his doubts are justified. But before then, two more murders have been committed and a third attempted . . .

GERALD VERNER

THE SQUEALER

Complete and Unabridged

LINFORD
Leicester

First published in Great Britain

First Linford Edition
published 2014

A catalogue record for this book is available
from the British Library.

ISBN 978–1–4448–1943–4

Published by
F. A. Thorpe (Publishing)
Anstey, Leicestershire

Set by Words & Graphics Ltd.
Anstey, Leicestershire
Printed and bound in Great Britain by
T. J. International Ltd., Padstow, Cornwall

This book is printed on acid-free paper

To
MESSRS. WRIGHT & BROWN
WITH EVERY GOOD WISH

Contents

1. The Curiosity of Mr. Sneath........1
2. Mr. Hake Makes an Appointment....................13
3. Murder!..............................23
4. Circumstantial Evidence 41
5. Peter Escott has a Visitor 55
6. Inspector Burnett is Doubtful.....65
7. The House of Death 78
8. The Mark on the Glass 91
9. Exit Mr. Sneath 108
10. A Visit to Mr. Hake...............126
11. A Drunken Woman................143
12. At The Bentley Buildings.........152
13. What the Night Watchman Saw 164
14. After the Inquest 174
15. The Press Cuttings................185
16. The Green Daimler 206

17. The House by the River.........219
18. Facing Death 233
19. Mr. Ginnings Takes a Hand......250
20. John Lane Explains 262
21. Broken Glass!.....................272
22. Vanished! 280
23. Betty Learns the Truth 289
24. The Sentence! 300
25. The Man Who Knew 310
26. The Grave in the Wood..........321
27. Frank Lane Behaves Strangely...330
28. The Midnight Meeting 342
29. Arrest! 351
30. A Scoop for the
    Megaphone.......................361

1

The Curiosity of Mr. Sneath

Mr. Sneath's besetting sin was an abnormal interest in other people's business. This little weakness of his had more than once caused considerable bodily damage to the person of Mr. Sneath. It had, on one occasion, been the cause of completely closing one of his small, shifty, and rather unpleasant eyes, and lost him two fairly respectable teeth. The long scar that reached from the middle of his right ear to the centre of his slightly receding chin was also a relic of this insatiable curiosity, and had been caused by the razor-sharp point of a knife held in the hand of one Abe Guiness, a gentleman of dubious reputation whose habits of acquiring with the aid of a brick, certain merchandise displayed in jewellers' shop windows, had brought him prominently to the notice of the police.

Mr. Sneath had been the means of introducing Mr. Guiness to Inspector Hadley, and Abe had not unreasonably been annoyed.

'You dirty little squealer!' he snarled in his rage, 'I'll rip you to pieces for this!'

He had attempted to put this threat into execution, but the detectives who had come to take him pulled him back.

Mr. Sneath, however, would carry the mark of Abe Guiness's knife to his grave.

The amount of money he had received for his information was not sufficiently large to compensate him for the pain of his wound, and for quite a long time after that Mr. Sneath gave up the dangerous and unpleasant occupation of police informer, and turned his talents to fresh fields and pastures new.

He eked out a not-very-certain livelihood by a little judicious blackmail, and the small side door at Scotland Yard which is known as the 'Traitors' Gate', through which, under cover of darkness, he had been wont to pass quite frequently, knew him no more.

Mr. Sneath lived in a small top room in

Rose Water Lane, Battersea, the narrowest and meanest street in that unsalubrious district.

Rose Water Lane had, so far as outward appearance went, no justification for its name. There were no roses in the vicinity and precious little water, if the sparing use of this commodity by the inhabitants of the lane was anything to go by.

Perhaps in the dim and distant past, Rose Water Lane had taken its twisting course through sweet-smelling meadows and grassy banks gay with wild flowers — perhaps there had even been rose-bushes growing on the brink of a cool pool somewhere near, but that must have been before the building of the gasworks.

An increasing population and the encroach of civilisation has covered what had been open country with row upon row of drab, smoke-grimed houses and factories, and now nothing remains of the sylvan beauties of the past except the park, which is the finest of its kind within the environs of greater London.

On a cold and wet November evening, after having fortified himself with a supper of bread and cheese and a large bottle of beer, Mr. Sneath descended the narrow and rickety staircase which led to his abode at the top of No. 6 and passed out into the darkness of the lane.

The unpleasantness of the night had driven the usual battalion of ragged, screaming children to seek the shelter of their dismal, disreputable homes, and the narrow thoroughfare was deserted except for an unusual object that was drawn up by the kerb a few yards on the right.

This was a small, closed car, and Mr. Sneath's thin lips curled into a twisted smile as he saw it, for it was the reason that had brought him out into the drizzle of rain that was still falling with monotonous regularity.

Mr. William Sneath had seen that car twice before, and in exactly the same place as it now stood, outside the blistered door of No. 26, and speculated as to why it was there.

Nobody residing at No. 26 had sufficient money to own a car like that — for it was an expensive make — nor did it seem likely that any of their friends would be in a position to either. But there the car was, and there it had been every Wednesday at precisely the same time for the past fortnight.

Mr. Sneath's uncontrollable curiosity had been definitely aroused. Something was going on at No. 26 that was unusual, and he wanted to know what it was.

Funds were very low. Every article that Mr. Sneath possessed that was in the smallest degree valuable — and these were not many — had found their way round the corner to the gentleman who carried on a lucrative business under the sign of three rather tarnished golden balls. Mr. Sneath's overcoat had been the last to go — a fact which was unpleasantly brought home to him by the rain which was soaking through his threadbare suit.

There was a small matter of overdue rent too, which his landlady had mentioned for the third time that day. Altogether things were not going well with Mr. Sneath, and something had to be done about it. Perhaps if he could find out the secret of the car's regular visits he might be able to turn it to his own advantage, and pick up a bit for himself.

He was pretty certain that whoever the visitor was, he came to see Frank Rabson, and he was equally certain that there was something peculiar going on. He noticed that Rabson had been very well-off lately. He had blossomed forth in several new suits, and had, only the previous night, changed a five-pound note over the bar of the Iron Pig; and five-pound notes were such a rarity in Rose Water Lane as to be practically unknown. He had refused a tentative suggestion on Mr. Sneath's part that ten shillings of the change would be of better use in Mr. Sneath's pocket than his own, and Mr. Sneath had not forgotten this refusal. Mr. Sneath objected strongly to people who refused him money when he needed it. From his point of view it was altogether wrong. He had ideas of his own regarding the financial situation as it applied to himself — ideas that were by no means conservative.

He made up his mind to find out the source of this sudden accession of wealth on the part of Mr. Frank Rabson. It was fishy, of that he was sure, and he thrived on other people's business that was fishy.

He shuffled along the streaming pavement, passed the waiting car, and went on until he came to the dark opening of a turning on the same side of the street. It was scarcely a yard wide, and its sides were composed of the high brick walls of two houses. It was, in fact, merely the break where one block of houses ended, and the next began, but Mr. Sneath knew that this narrow passage gave access to the back gardens of the houses on that side of the street of which No. 26 was one, and he was very interested in No. 26 just then.

It was pitch dark inside the alley, for the lamp which at one time had offered a feeble illumination had long since been broken by the inhabitants of the lane, who preferred darkness to light, but it was not the first time he had used this way, and he negotiated the narrow passage with ease.

The high walls only extended a short distance, and then gave place to low, wooden fences partially broken down, and like everything else in the neighbourhood, very much in need of repair. Mr. Sneath stopped by a portion of the fence that was rather more broken than the rest, and cautiously squeezed his way through into the square backyard beyond.

He paused for a moment, and then crossed the little concrete garden to the next fence. He climbed five in all before, according to his calculations, he arrived at the back of No. 26. The yard here was cleaner than the others, no rubbish littered the smooth concrete, and there had been an attempt to grow a few sickly and anaemic-looking flowers that struggled vainly to blossom amidst the smoke and grime.

Mr. Sneath, however, was not interested either in the neatness of the yard or the stunted chrysanthemums. What occupied his attention was the ray of light that streamed out between the crack in two curtains that had been pinned roughly across a window to the left of the back door.

Unless he was very much mistaken, the interview that he was desirous of participating in was taking place in the room from which that ray of light filtered out into the blackness of the night.

Mr. Sneath surveyed it thoughtfully.

Below was another window protected by rusty iron bars, whose lower half disappeared into a concrete-floored well that dropped some four feet below the level of the yard in which he stood.

Mr. Sneath rubbed the ginger bristles on his chin, and his narrow forehead contracted in a frown. It was a difficult proposition. The window with the badly drawn curtains was his objective, and its sill was a good foot above his head, for he was a short man. He could hear the faint hum of voices, but nothing that was being said. The question was how could he get a look into the room beyond, and also get close enough to hear what was going on? The narrow area was the trouble. It was a good three feet wide and there seemed no possibility of bridging the gap.

Mr. Sneath bent all his intelligence — which was not a great deal — towards solving this problem. He was determined to hear what was going on in that lighted room, and if possible see as well. He gazed slowly about him, taking stock of his surroundings, and presently a way out of his difficulty suggested itself. Leaning up against the wall by the back door was an old and dirty pair of steps. Mr. Sneath looked from these to the barred window, and decided on his plan of campaign. The bars rose from the concrete sill and were bolted to a flat piece of iron that was fastened into the brickwork at each side of the window, leaving a space of some six inches between the end of the bars and the curved top. With a great effort of concentration he reasoned that there was just room to wedge one end of the steps on the flat iron bar and the other on the ground, thus forming a bridge over the area from which he would be able to reach the sill of the window above.

He put this plan into execution, working quickly and noiselessly. He tested his improvised bridge, found that it bore his weight, and then, reaching up, he grasped the sill and drew himself up until he was perched precariously on the cracked stone slab.

The effort left him breathless, for Mr. Sneath was not used to such strenuous exercise, but when he recovered himself after a short rest he directed his attention to what was going on in the room into which he could see through the gap in the curtains.

There were two people sitting at the centre table, and the man facing him he recognised as Frank Rabson. The other was sitting with his back to the window, and, to Mr. Sneath's disappointment, he was unable to see his face. He wore a heavy raincoat, and, judging from the breadth of shoulder, Mr. Sneath came to the conclusion that he must be a man of unusual size. He was speaking rapidly in a high-pitched rather metallic voice, forming his words with scrupulous care, so that everything he said was clearly heard by the listener at the window, for a small, triangular piece of glass had become broken away at the bottom of one of the lower panes, and to this aperture Mr. Sneath glued his eager ear. His face as he listened, would have formed a study for an artist. Astonishment, greed and cunning chased themselves in rapid succession over his mean, unpleasant little face, and as the meaning of what he heard penetrated to his brain his small bead-like eyes glistened and his thin, sallow cheeks glowed, for here was something that, handled properly, ought to bring him affluence for life.

For over an hour he remained crouched on the sill, drinking in every word, and when, much later, he climbed stiffly down and hurried away in the darkness and the rain, he felt that at last his opportunity had come, and that he had stumbled on the chance of a fortune that seemed merely to require picking up.

Far into the night he sat in his little attic room thinking over what he had heard and laying his plans, his mind filled with the possibilities that the future held in store.

2

Mr. Hake Makes an Appointment

The offices of Messrs. Rand & Hake are at 304 Bedford Row. They are an old-established firm of solicitors, inasmuch as they have occupied the same suite of offices for a considerable number of years, and also for the fact that among their clients are to be found names that are more or less household words.

Of the original firm only Mr. Joshua Hake remained. Rand and the other Hake — the present one's father — had long since gone to wherever the partners of old-established firms of solicitors go when they die. The business was a very sound and respectable one — or, at least it had been until the present Mr. Hake had taken complete control. It is doubtful, however, if the satisfied and contented people whom Messrs. Rand & Hake numbered among their clientèle would have been quite so satisfied and contented if they could have got a glimpse of the small book which Mr. Joshua Hake kept locked in his private safe, and which showed certain dealings that were not traceable in the general books of the office. For Mr. Joshua Hake possessed an unfortunate liking for speculation and a further unfortunate habit of using other people's money to satisfy this liking.

There were many funds in Mr. Hake's trust that were not nearly so substantial as their owners imagined or as they had been when the senior partners were alive.

By judicious juggling of the accounts Mr. Hake had succeeded up to the present in keeping all the people whose wealth he had dipped into ignorant of the fact, and he was engaged in conducting a rather delicate little enterprise which, if successful, would have the effect of removing once and for all that unpleasant, volcano-like position in which he lived.

Neither Betty Hardy, his personal secretary, nor the aged and grey-haired clerk, who was as much a part of the office as the dusty deed-boxes which cluttered the shelves, knew anything about this lapse from rectitude on the part of their employer. To them Mr. Hake was a middle-aged gentleman, who lived a life of habit — rather dull, perhaps, but extremely respectable.

Betty liked him immensely. He was courteous and pleasant, and allowed many little favours to his staff. There were many afternoons when both the elderly clerk and the girl had been told that there was very little to do, and that if they liked they could leave early, and, not unnaturally, they put this down to Mr. Hake's generosity. In this, however, they were mistaken, for on these occasions Mr. Hake would receive into his comfortable inner office a visitor who never called when the staff were in attendance, and behind locked doors they would sit and talk about that scheme which was to relieve the solicitor from the unpleasant financial position in which he had succeeded in entangling himself.

On an evening nearly a week after Mr. Stephen Sneath's satisfactory expedition to the back of No. 26, Rose Water Lane, Mr. Hake sat in the padded chair behind his big desk and stared with frowning brow at the blotting-pad. He had the offices to himself, for Betty Hardy and the clerk had long since gone home.

Mr. Hake was a big man, not exactly fat, but largely built. He was big in every way: his huge hands, his enormous head, and great jutting nose; his mighty shoulders, were all outsize — all, that is, with the exception of his feet, and these were small and neat, and scarcely bigger than a woman's.

The expression of his face as he sat there lost in thought was worried, and one of his hands idly grasping a pencil kept up a ceaseless tattoo on the leather surface of the writing-table. Presently he sighed, laid down the pencil, and glanced at his watch. Rising, he crossed to the cupboard where he kept his overcoat, and put it on, adjusting a thick silk muffler carefully about his throat. With his usual methodical care — which was purely a matter of habit, for his mind was busily occupied with other things — he locked the door of his private office, passed through the outer office, and paused to lock the door giving on to the corridor also.

Putting his keys back into his pocket, he leisurely descended the stairs and came out into Bedford Row. The night was damp, but not actually raining. There was a suspicion of mist in the air, and Mr. Hake sought for the little box of throat tablets which it was his custom to carry about with him, and slipped one into his mouth. He was rather subject to colds.

He had to walk to the end of the row before he could find a taxi, and then saw one crawling towards him, and hailed it. Giving the driver instructions to take him to Piccadilly Circus, he clambered heavily inside, and settled himself comfortably in a corner.

Just before reaching the circus he tapped on the window, and the cab drew into the kerb. He opened the door and got out. It is a fact worthy of note, for it typifies Mr. Hake's character, that he gave the driver the exact fare as registered on the clock. Taking no notice of the man's by no means complimentary remarks, Mr. Hake walked slowly in the direction of the Eros Theatre, and under the portico in the front of the theatre he paused to glance at the photographs which extolled the delights that were to be found within.

He was still peering at an elaborate portrait of a number of young ladies dressed very sparingly, when there came a tap on his arm, and he turned to greet the man who had come silently up to his side.

'I got your message,' said the newcomer. 'Where can we talk? It's risky meeting in public like this. Why couldn't I have come to your office?'

'Because, my dear fellow,' said the solicitor, 'the cleaners will be there. Besides, nothing is really so private as the middle of a crowd. I suggest that we go to one of the more popular cafés — there is one just along the street.'

The other agreed, and they made their way towards the place Mr. Hake had suggested.

'What's happened?' asked his companion as they pushed their way through the throng.

'Something that's very disconcerting,' replied the solicitor. 'And not only disconcerting, but dangerous. It requires dealing with at once. That's why I asked you to meet me this evening.'

He refused to say any more until they were seated in an obscure corner of the all-night café, and the waitress had supplied them with the coffee that they had ordered. And then, with a glance round to assure himself that nobody was within hearing distance, he leaned forward and spoke rapidly in a low voice. The other listened intently, and his face grew grave as the solicitor continued.

'This is serious, very serious,' he commented, when Mr. Hake had eventually concluded. 'I must think.'

He stared at the table with knitted brows, unconsciously drawing little patterns on the marble surface with a burnt match. For nearly ten minutes he remained silent, and then suddenly breaking the match in half with a twist of his fingers, he looked across at the solicitor.

'There is only one thing to do,' he said. 'We must carry out our plans sooner than we intended. We were going to leave it for another three months, but now it must be done at once, not later than to-morrow night.'

Mr. Hake looked dubious.

'That doesn't give much time,' he said, shaking his head.

'I know it doesn't,' retorted the other, 'but it's got to be done. Our only difficulty is — who can we use?'

'You mean for the cat's-paw,' said the solicitor.

His companion nodded. 'Yes,' he replied. 'We've got to have somebody who's pretty well down and out. It shouldn't be difficult — the Embankment's swarming with them. Anyway, that's Rabson's business.'

'I think I can suggest somebody,' said Mr. Hake slowly. 'My — er — secretary, Miss Hardy' — he smiled gently as he mentioned the girl's name — 'is acquainted with a young man whom I think is at the moment having rather a bad time. She confided to me only a few days ago that this fellow — his name, if I remember rightly is Dick Mason — was out of a job, and asked me if I could recommend him to anybody. I took a note of his name and address, because after our last discussion, during which you suggested the method which was to be used, I thought he might be useful.'

'Excellent,' said the other. 'Rabson had better get in touch with him to-morrow without fail, and arrange that part of the business. You'll have to let me know as soon as he has fixed things. I must know for certain that everything is going without a hitch, otherwise I can't attend to my part of it.'

'I will get him to report to me at once,' said Mr. Hake, 'and as soon as he assures me definitely that everything is all right, I will communicate with you.'

For a long time they sat on talking, and when finally Mr. Hake took leave of his companion and looked round for a cab to take him home, the gloomy depression that had sat so heavily on him earlier in the evening had almost gone. And yet the conversation he had held in the tea-shop had sealed the fate of one man and placed another in the shadow of death!

3

Murder!

'I can't let it go on any longer, Mr. Mason. I got to live same as other people, and this 'ouse is my livin'. There's six weeks' rent owin' for your room, and I can't let it go on any longer.'

Mrs. Getteridge stood in the doorway of the small bed-sitting-room and looked at Dick Mason with a pair of red-rimmed and faded blue eyes.

'I'm very sorry' — he reddened and stammered in his embarrassment — 'very sorry indeed. I thought I should get that job I went after yesterday. I was hoping — '

''oping won't pay my bills,' broke in the landlady impatiently; 'and it won't pay your rent, neither. I've let you run on longer'n what I ought, and if you can't let me have what you owe me by this evening I shall 'ave to h'ask you to give up your room. I've already 'ad two people arter it.'

'All right, Mrs. Getteridge, I'll do my best.' He tried to impart a certain amount of hopefulness into his voice, but without much success. 'I had no idea I'd find it so difficult to get a job.'

'You certainly 'ave tried, I'll say that,' admitted Mrs. Getteridge grudgingly, 'and if things wasn't so bad — what with my 'usband out of work and young Jim in 'orspital — I wouldn't be so 'asty. But you know 'ow I'm placed. I ain't got nothing coming in 'cept what I makes out of the 'ouse, and by the time I've paid one thing and another there's precious little of that left.'

'I know.' Dick Mason picked up his hat. 'I'll do all I can to let you have some money this evening.'

'Well, unless you do you'll 'ave to go,' said the landlady definitely.

'It ain't no good you comin' back without it and makin' excuses, and I mean what I says.' She gave a curt nod as if to emphasise that this was her final word, and took her departure.

He waited until the sound of her heavy

feet had faded away into the lower regions, and then went down the narrow stairs into the street.

Crator Street was one of those innumerable turnings that lie at the back of Tottenham Court Road, and after pausing irresolutely on the pavement, Mason bent his steps towards the main thoroughfare. He had not the least idea of where he was going or what he was going to do, but something had to be done unless he wanted to spend the night sleeping on the Embankment. The clothes he stood up in, a sum of twopence halfpenny, and a battered trunk containing a few items of clothing constituted his sole worldly possessions. And he owed Mrs. Getteridge close on eight pounds.

It was a bright, sunny morning, with a fresh tang to the air that brought a glow to the cheeks, but none of the brightness was reflected in Dick Mason's lean face as he walked dejectedly along, envying the stream of people hurrying to work. A few months ago he had been among them holding down a fairly comfortable, if not very lucrative, job in a firm of stock-brokers in the City. The slump, however, had forced them to cut down their staff, and he had had to go, in company with several others. His salary had left very little margin to save on, but he had managed to put by a few pounds. The meagre little nest-egg, however, had dwindled to nothing, and his ceaseless search for work had been unrewarded.

He came out at the junction of Tottenham Court Road and Oxford Street, and swung off down New Oxford Street, his objective being Fleet Street, where he could look through the advertisements in the morning papers in the rather vain hope of finding something in the nature of a job. Passing a side-turning that would have taken him to Bedford Row, his thoughts turned to Betty Hardy. That little romance looked like flickering out. Not through any fault of the girl's — she had been a brick, and had offered more than once to lend him money — but because his pride refused to allow him to tie her down to anything definite in the circumstances.

They had met a little more than a year ago, and mutual liking had developed rapidly into something stronger. A tentative engagement had resulted, and then had come his unexpected dismissal and the shattering of the dream.

Thinking of Betty Hardy occupied his time until he reached Fleet Street, and then for the rest of the morning he went from office to office searching diligently among the advertisement columns of the various papers for something that would suit him. By one o'clock he had noted three possibles, and since they were all within walking distance, he decided to call personally as soon as he judged that the heads of the different concerns had returned from lunch. He was feeling really hungry himself, for he had had no breakfast, and his last meal had consisted of two pennyworth of chip potatoes at nine o'clock on the previous night. However, one cannot get much in the way of food for twopence halfpenny, and so, after thinking it over, he entered a tobacconist's and invested the last of his capital in a packet of Woodbines and a box of matches. The cigarettes would at least allay the pangs of hunger and help to soothe his nerves.

There is a small patch of garden under the shadow of St. Paul's, where it is possible to sit for a while if one is lucky enough to find a vacant seat, and Dick was lucky. It was the only piece of luck he had had for a long time, and here he smoked two of his cigarettes and surveyed his unpleasant position from all angles.

At three o'clock he decided to make the calls on the firms he had selected, and set off on this uncongenial task.

At the first he was greeted with a curt intimation that all applicants were expected to write, and that no interviews could be granted without an appointment. At the second, after he had waited for over an hour and a half, he eventually saw the managing clerk, a supercilious individual who took all his particulars and promised to let him know. By the time he had reached the last one the job had already gone.

Weary and dispirited, he came out of the big block of offices, and mechanically turned his steps westward. He was feeling sick and a little dizzy, and the roar of the traffic sounded a long way off.

It was useless going back to his lodgings, although he was walking in that direction. Mrs. Getteridge had meant what she had said. Unless he could take some money home with him, the night would find him without a home. And he had not a cent, or the slightest prospect of getting one. He had no relations and few friends — none whom he felt inclined to go to for help, or who would have helped him, for that matter, if he had.

There was Betty Hardy, certainly. The smallest hint of his position to her would, he knew, at once bring material assistance. But his whole being revolted at the very idea. He might have sunk low, but not low enough to sponge on a woman. In this, although he did not know it, he was revealing the slight weakness in his character which was his main fault. There is only one justification for refusing the loan of money from anybody under certain circumstances, and that is the absolute certainty that you will never be in a position to pay it back. The fact that Dick had refused the offers which Betty Hardy had, from time to time, made him showed that he had reached that stage when he never expected to be able to pull himself out of the rut of unemployment, and earn sufficient money, over and above his living expenses, to pay her back.

Force of habit brought him eventually to the corner of Crator Street, and it was with a start of surprise that he discovered where he was. He was debating with himself whether to go in and tell Mrs. Getteridge that it was impossible for him to find her the rent that he owed, and ask her to give him a few days longer, when a man who had been slowly walking up and down on the opposite side of the road saw him, and, quickening his pace, came towards him.

'Would you like to earn ten pounds?' The voice, almost in his ear, made Dick swing round and stare at his questioner incredulously.

'Were — were you speaking to me?' he asked a little dazedly.

The man who had accosted him nodded briefly. 'Yes,' he answered curtly. 'I said, would you like to earn ten pounds?'

'Are you joking?' said Dick, eyeing him up and down, for he was shabbily dressed in a soiled waterproof and a greasy bowler hat, and certainly did not look as though he possessed ten pence, much less the amount he mentioned.

The other shook his head. 'No,' he replied, 'I'm perfectly serious.'

'Then show me how I can earn it,' said Mason, 'and as long as it's honest, I'm your man.'

The man in the bowler hat shot a quick glance up and down the street. 'It's honest enough,' he said quickly, 'but we can't talk here. There's a tea-shop just round the corner; let's go along there.'

Without waiting for a reply, he set off, and Dick followed, his mind in a whirl.

If this turned out to be genuine it was the greatest piece of luck that had ever happened. With ten pounds he could settle with Mrs. Getteridge, and still have enough to keep himself going for a bit, and surely before that was gone he could manage to find some sort of job.

They reached the tea-shop, and his companion pushed open the swing door and made his way to a secluded table, motioning Dick to a seat by his side.

While he gave the order for tea and toast to the waitress, Dick covertly took stock of him, and the result was anything but reassuring.

The man was a most unprepossessing specimen of humanity. His face was long and thin, with a wide slit of a mouth that seemed to have slipped to one side. Above the long upper lip his nose tilted upwards, and across the bridge was a scar — a deep cicatrix — that gave it the appearance of being nearly cut in half. His eyes were small, and the left one had a drooping lid that made him look as though he was constantly winking, which, together with his lopsided mouth, gave to his face a peculiar leering expression even in his most serious moments.

He spoke no word until the tea had

been served, and then, gulping a mouthful of the steaming fluid, and pushing a packet of cigarettes across to his companion, he leaned forward.

'Do you know 'igh Wycombe?' he asked.

Dick, his mouth full of toast, shook his head.

'Humph!' The other gave a grunt. 'Oh, well, it doesn't matter. You can't mistake the place I want you to go to, anyway. It's the biggest house in the district.'

'You want me to go to High Wycombe?' said Mason, reaching for a second slice of toast, and munching it eagerly.

'Yes, to a place called Maddox Court,' said the other. 'Look here, I'll tell you as much as I can about the business. I'm working for a firm of private detectives — Ford & Earley, I expect you've heard of 'em — and we're doing a job for Sir James Maddox, who lives at Maddox Court. I can't tell you what it is — it's a confidential matter — but I've got a letter 'ere' — he took an envelope from his pocket and laid it on the marble-topped table — 'which has got to be delivered to

Sir James to-night. If you'll deliver it there's ten quid for you.'

Dick looked at the envelope, and then from it to the man facing him.

'It seems a lot of money for such a simple job,' he said suspiciously after a pause. 'A district messenger would take it for a few shillings. What's the idea?'

'A district messenger is likely to talk,' said the representative of Messrs. Ford & Earley, 'and Sir James wants the whole thing kept private. I don't mind telling you that there's very grave issues at stake — and there's another thing. This letter 'as got to be delivered into Sir James's own hands without the risk of the household knowing anything about it.'

'That sounds rather a tall order,' said Dick, raising his eyebrows. 'How do you suppose I should manage that?'

'I'll tell you that,' was the reply, 'when you tell me that you're going to do the job.'

Dick considered. The whole business was queer, very queer, but ten pounds was ten pounds, and anyhow it was no concern of his what lay at the back of the matter. There was nothing criminal in delivering a letter. Although the man beside him looked seedy and shabbily dressed his voice held a note of authority, and after all, if he was representing a firm of private detectives, there was the distinct possibility that the clothes were merely a disguise. A vision of Mrs. Getteridge rose before his eyes and decided him.

'Carry on,' he said briefly. 'I'll take the letter.'

'Good!' The other drank the remainder of his tea and pushed aside the cup. 'Now listen. Sir James is expecting the letter and will be waiting in 'is study at twelve o'clock to-night to receive it. 'is study is on the ground floor, and 'as a pair of French windows that open into the garden. He is leaving these unfastened and that is the way you'll enter the 'ouse. Do you understand?'

Dick nodded.

'You will time yourself,' the other continued, 'so that you get there exactly at twelve, neither before nor after, for that is the time Sir James has arranged to be alone. If you reach the place before twelve you must hang about until twelve strikes. Don't forget that; it's most important. There's a path about halfway up the main drive that leads round to the study windows, and all you've got to do is to push them open and go in. There is no need to knock. You will then give Sir James the letter and leave. That's all. Quite simple, ain't it?' Dick nodded again.

'It seems simple enough,' he agreed.

'Right!' The man in the bowler hat took a shabby note-case from his pocket. 'Here's a pound for expenses. Meet me in 'ere to-morrow morning at ten-twenty, and I'll give you the other nine quid I promised you.'

He flicked the note towards Dick, and snapped his fingers for the waitress.

'Don't forget,' he said in a low voice. 'It's important that you get to Maddox Court exactly at twelve.'

'All right.' Dick picked up the money and the envelope. 'I'll remember. And I shall see you here in the morning?'

'Yes, ten-twenty without fail,' replied the other.

The waitress came up in answer to his summons and he waited in silence while the girl made out the cheque, and when she had gone, rose.

'I must go back to the office now, and report,' he said. 'Good-bye, and carry out my instructions exactly.'

Dick watched him stride across the half-empty shop, pay the bill at the cash-desk, and go out. And then he set about ordering the first real meal he had for days. During its consumption he thought over the remarkable errand that lay in front of him, and in spite of the old saying that coming events cast their shadows before them, no shadow reached him to warn him of the terrible result of that journey, or the dire peril into which it was to land him.

He reached High Wycombe at a little after eleven-thirty, and inquired the way to Maddox Court from the ticket collector at the station. The house was apparently quite close, for the official was voluble in his directions, and offered the information that it was only about ten minutes' walk. A giant might have walked it in that time, but it took Dick every second of twenty minutes before he came to the drive gates, and turned into the dark avenue of leafless chestnuts.

The night was very dark. There was no moon, and heavy clouds obscured the sky, shutting out even the feeble rays of the stars, and it was with some difficulty that he located the side path that had been described to him, and following its twisting course presently came in sight of a pair of lighted french windows. As he caught sight of them he thought he heard a slight sound from a clump of shrubbery behind him, the rustle of leaves and the scrape of a foot on gravel. He swung round quickly. For a moment or two he listened intently, but the sound was not repeated, and he concluded that it was either his imagination or had been made by some animal moving about among the bushes.

Dismissing it from his mind, he turned his attention once more to the lighted windows in front of him.

One of them was ajar, and when he drew closer and tried to peer into the room beyond he found that heavy curtains obscured his vision. And then, for the first time, it occurred to him that he had no means of telling the time. His watch had long since gone the way of his other possessions. How was he going to be certain when it was twelve? Even as he wondered a clock somewhere in the distance began to strike the hour. He waited until the last note had died away on the still night air, and then, hesitating for a fraction of a second, he took the letter from his pocket and pushed the window further open.

Stepping across the threshold, he pulled aside the obscuring curtains beyond.

And then he stopped dead, his eyes wide, and the blood draining from his face, for the only occupant of the large room lay sprawled on the floor almost at his feet, his grey head dappled a horrid crimson which was spreading in an ugly patch over the carpet. With a cry that came no farther than his suddenly-parched throat, Dick took a step forward. The man was dead. There was no doubt about that. His contorted face and staring eyes were more convincing than any doctor's verdict, and the manner of his death, too, was clearly evident. He had been struck down by the twisted steel poker that lay by his side.

Overwhelmed with horror and scarcely realising what he was doing, Dick stooped and picked the stained thing up, and then he heard a noise behind him and swung round. He caught the merest glimpse of a shadowy figure with upraised arm, and then something soft and heavy crashed down on his head. The whole scene split into a whirl of blinding light, and blackness swallowed up his senses!

4

Circumstantial Evidence

To this day Dick Mason is unable to say how long he remained unconscious. That it was not very long was subsequently proved at the inquest. He came to himself with a throbbing head, struggled to his knees, and then clutching a table for support staggered unsteadily to his feet. The shock of his discovery followed by the blow had rendered him incapable of clear thought. His mind was a chaotic whirlpool of fragmentary pieces. The man in the tea-shop — the letter — the dead man on the floor . . .

He tried to force his brain to work normally, tried by an effort of will to check the buzzing that was like the rapid pulsation of a steam hammer, but without success. A sub-conscious warning voice was telling him to get away from this room with its horrid occupant — to leave while he had yet time. But his feet were shod with leaden weights, and the slightest movement sent the whole place whirling round him!

As through a mist he saw a door at the far end suddenly open, heard faintly the startled cry of the man who entered, found himself gripped roughly by strong hands, and realised with a shock that he still held that horrible, twisted steel thing with which the man on the floor had been done to death.

The strong hands forced him into a chair, and he heard a voice calling loudly, and then other voices excited and shrill. He caught a glimpse of a pale, fair-haired girl in a low-cut frock of some black material, and then everything faded into a jumbled mass of sights and sounds out of which nothing emerged clearly, and of which he was unable to remember anything.

His first positive recollection, after this second lapse into semi-unconsciousness, was of a stout, red-faced man who was standing in front of him and talking to him. The deep voice of this individual seemed to come from a long way off, but eventually it became clearer, and Dick discovered that he was being asked his name.

He tried twice unsuccessfully to answer, and when, at the third attempt, he did manage to stammer out a reply his voice was harsh and cracked and utterly unlike his own.

'Dick Mason.'

The large, red-faced man made a note in the open book he was holding in his hand.

'Where do you live?' he said.

'14 Crator Street,' muttered Dick, raising a shaking hand to his head to try and still the dull ache which throbbed behind his eyes.

'What have you got to say for yourself?' went on the voice of the red-faced man. 'How did you come here, and what was your motive for this crime?'

Dick stared at him dully, and then it became borne in on his dazed senses that he was being accused of having killed the grey-haired man on the floor! The knowledge acted like a douche of cold water. It collected his scattered wits and bunched them up together.

'I — I know nothing about this business at all,' he cried. 'The man was already dead when I got here.'

'That's all nonsense,' broke in a tall man in evening-dress who was standing beside the red-faced man. 'You were crouching over the body with the poker in your hand when I came into the room and discovered you.'

'But I never killed him,' repeated Dick. 'He was like that when I found him.'

He saw the red-faced man exchange a glance with the other.

'I think we had better hear his story, Mr. Stroude,' he said, 'although I've not much doubt myself. Now then' — he looked at Dick keenly — 'if you didn't commit this murder, what were you doing here at all at twelve o'clock at night?'

'I came with a letter for Sir James Maddox,' Dick explained. 'I was told to come by way of the french windows and to deliver it to him personally at twelve o'clock.'

The red-faced man grunted sceptically.

'A letter,' he echoed. 'Who was it from?'

'A firm of private detectives, Ford & Earley,' said Dick, and he related his meeting with the man in the bowler hat, and the subsequent arrangement in the tea-shop.

The red-faced man listened without comment, but it was obvious from his expression that he did not believe a word of it. Neither, apparently, did the man whom he had addressed as Stroude, for he broke in again almost before Dick had finished.

'I've never heard such a lot of nonsense,' he said. 'Sir James Maddox had not employed any firm of private detectives. I was his secretary, and completely in his confidence; I should have known if he had, Inspector, and I have heard nothing about it.'

'It sounds rather a thin story to me,' admitted the inspector, 'particularly the bit about having been struck on the head by some unknown person almost immediately on entering this room.'

'I swear it's the truth,' exclaimed Dick. 'The man who was representing Ford &

Earley told me that Sir James Maddox wished the whole matter treated with the utmost secrecy — that very grave issues were at stake. That was why he wanted me to deliver the letter instead of giving it to a district messenger, as I suggested. It was to be delivered to Sir James Maddox without the knowledge of the rest of the household.'

'Well, we can soon prove whether you're speaking the truth or not,' said the inspector. 'I've heard of Messrs. Ford & Earley, they're a very reputable firm, and we can get on the 'phone to them first thing in the morning, and hear what they've got to say. In the meanwhile, I'm afraid you'll have to consider yourself under arrest, and I must warn you that anything you say will be taken down, and may be used in evidence against you.'

He made a sign to a uniformed constable, who had been hovering in the background, and the man stepped across and took up his position behind Dick's chair.

'If the man's speaking the truth,' said Stroude, 'where is the letter he mentions?

It should be either in his pocket or somewhere in the room.'

'A very good point.' The inspector smiled at the secretary. 'We'll see if we can find it.'

He approached Dick, and with deft fingers, made a thorough search of his pockets. When he had finished he straightened up shaking his large head.

'Not a sign of it,' he remarked, and the tone of his voice intimated that that was exactly what he had expected.

'It must be in the room somewhere,' said Dick. 'I had the thing in my hand, when I came in through the window.'

The inspector made a diligent search.

'It's not here,' he declared. 'I never expected it would be.'

'Then it must have been taken by the man who hit me,' exclaimed Dick. 'I tell you I had it in my — '

'Oh, yes, we know all about that,' said the inspector sternly. 'I may as well tell you candidly that I don't believe this letter ever existed any more than I believe in the existence of the man who is supposed to have knocked you out.'

'But surely there's sufficient proof of that,' remonstrated Dick. 'Mr. Stroude will tell you — he must tell you — that I was only just recovering consciousness when he came into the room.'

'Yes, that's quite true, Inspector,' admitted Stroude. 'But it's my belief that in his hurry to escape he slipped on the polished floor and fell, striking his head against that table.'

He nodded his head towards a heavy oak table that stood in the alcove by the window.

'If you look at the floor over there,' he went on, 'you'll see that there's a long scratch, that might easily have been made by the heel of his boot.'

'I had already seen that,' said the inspector who had done nothing of the sort, 'and had come to the same conclusion as you. Personally I think it's a pretty clear case, and when we've tested the weapon for finger-prints and heard what Messrs. Ford & Earley have got to say we shall have all the proof that we require.'

He shut up his note-book with a snap

and returned it to his pocket.

'I'll be getting back to the station now, sir,' he continued. 'I'll have the body removed to one of the upstairs rooms, and it will be necessary to have this room locked and a constable left on guard. It's a dreadful business. I hope you will convey my deepest sympathy to the dead man's daughter.'

'Thank you, Inspector,' said Stroude. 'She is, naturally, at the moment dreadfully upset. It's something, however, to have caught the man responsible.'

'But I'm not responsible,' cried Dick. 'I never did it — I swear I never did it!'

'We'll have to leave that to the jury to decide,' said the inspector, and he prepared to take his leave.

The rest of the night seemed to Dick like a nightmare. He was handcuffed and taken from Maddox Court in a ramshackle Ford to the police station at High Wycombe, where, after the usual preliminaries had been completed, he was locked in a small, cold, and uncomfortable cell, and left alone with his unpleasant thoughts.

He was in a very serious position. Now that he was able to think the matter over clearly he saw how very difficult it would be to prove that he had had no hand in that dreadful crime. The only possible hope was that the man who had sent him to deliver the letter would come forward. He brightened a little as he thought of this — of course the man would come forward. As soon as the police got into communication with Messrs. Ford & Earley they would learn that in that respect at least he had been telling the truth. The man in the bowler hat could bear witness that a letter had been given him to deliver to Sir James Maddox and the fact that that letter could not be found would make his story concerning the presence of the man who had struck him down more probable.

As these thoughts occurred to him he began to feel more cheerful, and presently, thoroughly tired out, he settled himself on the plank bed with which the cell was provided and fell asleep.

The grey light of dawn was streaming through the narrow barred window when the rattle of a key in the lock awakened him, and he sat up as the red-faced inspector came in. He was accompanied by a constable, and carried in his hand a small box, out of which he took some sheets of paper and an ink-pad.

'I want your finger-prints,' he said gruffly, and proceeded to take a careful impression of the tip of each of Dick's fingers and his thumbs.

He looked at the result of his labours and nodded. 'Do you still intend to stick to your story?' he asked, raising his eyes, at last, and looking at Dick.

'Most certainly I do,' replied Dick. 'It's the truth.'

'Humph! Well, you'll have some difficulty in proving it,' said the Inspector. 'I may as well tell you that we have tested the poker, and the only prints on it are yours!'

Dick stared at him incredulously. 'That's impossible,' he cried, 'I — '

'Impossible or not,' broke in the inspector, 'it's a fact, and facts are the only things that count. If you take my advice you'll make a clean breast of it and save a lot of trouble.'

'I shall do nothing of the sort,' replied Dick. 'I am not guilty.'

The inspector shrugged his shoulders.

'Well, if you won't take my advice, you won't,' he said. 'But I can tell you you won't get away with that story of yours — it's much too thin. I can't force you to say anything that's likely to incriminate yourself, but I should think it over well if I were you.'

He turned and was on the point of leaving the cell when Dick stopped him.

'Can I have permission to telephone a friend?' he asked.

'That depends,' said the inspector dubiously. 'Who is he, what's his name?'

Dick smiled. 'It's not a he,' he replied. 'I want to 'phone a lady. If you insist on keeping me here I have a right to arrange for someone to look after my defence.'

'You're allowed to have a lawyer to attend to your interests if that's what you mean,' said the inspector.

'That's exactly what I mean,' answered Dick. 'I want to get in touch with this lady so that she can arrange something for me.'

'I shall have to be present while you telephone,' warned the red-faced man, and Dick nodded.

'I'm quite agreeable to that,' he said, 'and I don't want to 'phone until after nine. It's no good trying before then.'

'All right,' said the inspector. 'You can 'phone at nine. I'll arrange for you to be brought into the charge-room just after that hour.'

He left the cell, and the door was shut and locked behind him. At a quarter-past nine a constable appeared and conducted Dick to the charge-room.

The red-faced inspector was standing in front of the fire, and he jerked his head towards the telephone that stood on the sergeant's desk.

'There you are,' he said briefly, and crossing over, Dick picked up the receiver.

He gave the number of Messrs. Rand & Hake's offices and waited for the exchange to connect him. And that telephone message was destined to have far-reaching results, for it was eventually to lead to the unmasking of a very clever plot.

5

Peter Escott Has a Visitor

Peter Escott became a crime reporter by accident. This is literally true, for the accident was caused by Ted Ackland, whose speciality was the manufacture of 'snide' half crowns, and whose favourite weapon was a short length of shot-filled rubber tubing. Peter was at that time a junior reporter on the *Megaphone*, and had gone down to Deptford to try and get a story from the man who had just won the first prize in that enterprising paper's Crossword Competition.

He had spent the entire afternoon in trying to find this elusive individual, and had eventually run him to earth in a public-house near Tanners Hill, where he was celebrating his good fortune with large quantities of beer. By this time he was not in a condition to give an interview to anybody, and Peter left rather disgusted at having had all his trouble for nothing. On his way back to the road where he could catch his bus, he had to pass through a rather dingy narrow street, and halfway along this he came upon a knot of shouting, struggling men. Apparently there was a free fight in progress, and scenting the possibility of a story that might appease the hard heart of the news editor who was awaiting the result of his interview with the prize-winner, Peter went over to see what was happening.

It was at that moment that Ted Ackland succeeded in breaking away from the plain-clothes man who held him, and made a dash for freedom. He dashed straight into the arms of Peter, and being under the impression that he was another of his natural enemies, the police, used the 'cosh' which he carried in his hand to good effect.

Peter woke up in a hospital bed, a little uncertain as to what had occurred, but acutely conscious that his head was extremely painful, and that it felt at least six sizes too large for him. To him later in the day came Chief Inspector Trimmer, a thin, cadaverous man, whose mournful face would have made his fortune as an undertaker.

In a rather monotonous voice he told Peter all about Ted Ackland, who appeared to have spent the greater part of his life in prison, and was anyway certain to spend the next three years there.

'He might have got away if it hadn't been for you,' said Mr. Trimmer, shaking his head dolefully. 'But bumpin' into you delayed him, an' we got him.'

Peter assured the inspector that he was very glad to have been of assistance, and from that day a close friendship sprang up between the melancholy police official and the young reporter.

When he had nothing else to do he would drop into Scotland Yard and chat to his friend, and Mr. Trimmer in his lugubrious way would welcome him. It became a habit with him to call on the inspector at any hour of the day or night, for that gentleman was nearly always to be found sitting in his bare, rather cheerless office smoking an apparently limitless supply of Woodbines, which, so far as Peter had been able to discover, was his one and only amusement.

It is almost certain that somewhere in London Mr. Trimmer had a home, and a bed, but he seldom went to either, and nobody had the least idea of their location. This may have accounted for his habitual expression of tiredness. Peter asked him once if he ever slept, and the inspector shook his head gloomily.

'Very seldom,' he answered. 'Suffered from in-whatever-you-call-it ever since I was a boy. I'm all right if I get a nap every now an' again.'

From his acquaintance with Mr. Trimmer, Peter was able to pick up a lot of useful information. So much so that his speciality in turning in good crime stories for the *Megaphone* came under the notice of the news editor.

'You gone in for criminology, Escott?' asked that harassed man one day when the reporter turned in the 'copy' for a smash-and-grab raid on a West End jewellers. 'For the last few months I've had more crime stuff from you than from anyone else on the paper.'

Peter explained and the news editor grunted.

'H'm, if you go on like this, you'll be cutting out Dringer,' he said, and his words were prophetic. For when Herbert Dringer, the *Megaphone's* star crime man, left to go to another paper, Peter was offered his job.

A good reporter is born and not made. He must have a nose for news which nothing but sheer instinct can give him. And he must be prepared to subordinate everything for his paper. The faculty of being able to 'smell' out a story is his greatest asset, and this cannot be cultivated. It either is, or it isn't, and Peter possessed this faculty to an abnormal degree. He lived in a microscopic flat consisting of two rooms and a bath off Great Russell Street. There was also a kitchen, according to the landlord, but this was so tiny that it was quite easily overlooked on a first visit. It was, however, quite large enough for Peter's requirements, for he seldom had more than his breakfast at home.

He had come home early one afternoon

and was making himself a cup of tea when he received his unexpected visit from Betty Hardy. It had been a particularly unpleasant day. In the morning there had been a thick fog which had given place to an incessant drizzle that looked like continuing all night. He was surprised to see the girl, but he ushered her into the small sitting-room, and eyed her slim figure in its neat green mackintosh with appreciative eyes.

Betty Hardy was very pretty. Her soft brown hair which escaped from under the close-fitting hat she wore, framed a face that most people looked at twice. Even now, with the trouble that clouded her grey eyes, she brought an extra brightness into the rather dingy room. His meeting with her had been the result of another accident. She had been trying to board a crowded bus in Fleet Street, and had been elbowed off in the rush. But for Peter's presence immediately behind her she would have fallen, but he had managed to catch her just in time. They were both going the same way, for he was returning to his flat and she was going back to the offices of Messrs. Rand and Hake, and so they travelled together in the next bus that came along.

There was nothing akin to love in the friendship which had sprung up between them from this chance meeting. He knew all about Dick Mason, and had met and liked him. Peter had, in fact, done his best to get him a job, but without success. He was surprised to see the girl, for this was the first time she had visited him, but he saw at once by the expression of her face that something was the matter. She seemed a little nervous, and he hastened to put her at her ease.

'Sit down and make yourself at home, Betty,' he said cheerfully, pushing forward a chair nearer the gas fire. 'If you wait half a second I'll get you a cup of tea.'

He hurried into the little kitchenette where the kettle was boiling furiously, made the tea and carried it back on a tray into the sitting-room.

The girl had discarded her streaming waterproof and was sitting with her wet shoes stretched out towards the fire.

'Listen, Peter,' she said as he came in, 'I

want to talk to you. I'm terribly worried.'

'I thought there was something the matter,' he said as he poured out the tea. 'What is it?'

'It's about Dick,' she began, as she stripped the gloves she had forgotten to take off, and folded them mechanically into a ball. 'I don't know quite how to begin, but — but there was a murder committed last night, and they've arrested Dick for it. He didn't do it, Peter, I'm sure he didn't do it!'

The words came out in a rush, and then her self-control gave way and she began to cry, dabbing at her eyes with a ridiculous wisp of handkerchief. It was some time before Peter succeeded in calming her, and then slowly in halting phrases and monosyllables, he persuaded her to tell her story.

'He got permission to telephone me at the office,' she concluded breathlessly, 'and I went to see him, and he told me the story of the man and the letter. But the police don't believe him; they say he's just making it up. Will you try and do something, Peter? You know them, and they may listen to you.'

'Of course I'll do anything I can, Betty,' he answered quickly. 'My God, what a rotten position!' His forehead wrinkled in thought. 'The first thing I'd better do is to try and see Mason. Luckily I know Burnett.'

He crossed over to his desk and picked up the telephone directory. After a few minutes he found the number he was seeking and put the call through. Presently he was talking to Inspector Burnett at the police station at High Wycombe. The conversation was a lengthy one, but eventually he hung up the receiver, and when he turned away from the instrument his face was very grave.

'The police haven't any doubt about Mason's guilt,' he said. 'No letter was found on him when he was searched to bear out his story, and the only fingerprints on the weapon that killed Sir James Maddox were his.'

'The letter must have been taken from him by the person who struck him down, just after he had discovered the crime,' said Betty quickly, 'and he admitted he had picked up the poker.'

Peter nodded, and his frown deepened.

'Our difficulty will be to convince the police of that,' he said. 'They regard his story as a pack of lies from beginning to end. So far as I can see the only way to prove that he has been speaking the truth is to find the man who sent him to Maddox Court with that letter.'

'How can you do that?' asked the girl anxiously.

'I don't know,' he answered. 'Perhaps I'll be able to pick on something when I get to High Wycombe.'

'It is good of you, Peter — ' she began gratefully, but he cut her short.

'You can thank me when I've done something,' he said with a grin, 'and anyway, I'm the one to be grateful. You've put me on to a good story.'

He went out into the hall and came back with his hat and coat.

'Now,' he said, 'you cut along home, and I'll let you know directly I've got any news.'

6

Inspector Burnett is Doubtful

Darkness had closed down on the greyness of the day when Peter brought his dilapidated little car to a standstill outside the police station at High Wycombe. There was a constable on duty at the entrance and he came forward as the reporter got down.

'Are you Mr. Escott?' he enquired and when Peter nodded, 'Inspector Burnett is expecting you. You'll find him in the charge room.'

He entered the police station, and a short, thick-set, red-faced man, who was standing in front of the fire, looked round and held out his hand in greeting.

'Hullo, Peter,' he said in a rather deep, pleasant voice. 'Haven't seen you for some time. How are you getting on?'

'Fine!' answered the reporter, and gave the other a firm grip. 'I suppose you think

I'm an awful nuisance, Burney.'

The inspector smiled. 'You're not such a nuisance as some of 'em,' he answered. 'What do you want to know?'

'Everything,' answered Peter. 'Apart from the *Megaphone* I've got a private interest in this business.'

He told the inspector what it was, and Burnett pursed his lips in a silent whistle. 'I think you're going to have all your work cut out,' he said. 'The evidence against Mason is pretty damning.'

'Well, I can only do my best,' replied Peter. 'To start with I should like to ask you one or two questions, and also get Mason's story at first hand, if possible.'

'There'll be no difficulty about that,' answered Burnett. 'I'll be only too pleased to supply you with all the help I can. But if you're going to try and prove that this fellow isn't guilty, I'm afraid you'll find that you're only wasting your time.' He shook his head doubtfully. 'It's a clear enough case. I've never seen a clearer.'

'Sometimes they turn out to be the most obscure,' said the reporter. 'Up to now, of course, I've only heard the barest outline. Perhaps you'd run over the whole thing in detail for me.'

'That won't take very long,' said the inspector. 'As I said before, it's obvious enough.' He pulled forward a chair, and invited the reporter to sit down, and then leaning comfortably back against the mantelpiece, he began a clear account of the tragedy that had occurred at Maddox Court.

'It was about ten minutes past twelve when we first got the news of the murder,' he said. 'Miss Maddox, that's the dead man's daughter, rung up to say that her father had been found dead in his study, and that Mr. Stroude, his secretary, was holding the man who had committed the crime. I happened to be here, luckily, when the message came through, finishing some reports, and I went up to Maddox Court at once, calling for Dr. Taylor, who is the police surgeon of this district, on my way. I found Sir James lying on the floor of his study stone dead, and Stroude standing guard over this fellow Mason.

'Sir James had been killed with the

poker from the fireplace, and a particularly brutal crime it was too. The doctor said he could not have been dead very long because the body was still warm, and there were no signs of rigor mortis. Stroude, who discovered the crime, said he came into the study at about five minutes past twelve with some work that he'd been doing for Sir James, and which his employer had particularly asked should be finished that night before he went to bed. He had been horrified to find him dead, and Mason staring down at him in a dazed condition. He at once alarmed the house, and while Miss Maddox rang up the police station, he looked after Mason to see that he didn't get away.'

'Did he try to get away?' interjected Peter.

The inspector shook his head. 'No,' he replied. 'He seemed too dazed by what he had done. He was in a half-conscious state, and just sat and stared at the floor.'

'A state that could also be accounted for by his story of having been struck on the head by some unknown man,' remarked the reporter.

'There's no doubt that he'd received a blow,' admitted the inspector, 'but I don't think he got it in the way he said. However, I'm coming to that. I questioned Mason, and he told me this story of the man who had sent him with the letter. According to him he had never seen this fellow before, but the man had met him at the end of Crator Street where Mason lives, and offered him ten pounds to take this letter to Sir James at twelve. The man told him he was working for Messrs. Ford and Earley, private enquiry agents, but I've been on the 'phone to them and they know nothing about it at all. Sir James Maddox had never engaged them to do any work for him of any kind. Mason says this unknown man instructed him to go round to the french windows leading into the study at exactly twelve o'clock, push them open and deliver the letter to Sir James, who would be waiting for it and expecting it. Mason swears that he carried out these instructions, and that when he got there found Sir James already dead on the floor.

'He had just picked up the poker with which the crime was committed when somebody struck him down from behind, and he lost his senses. He can give no description whatever of this unknown man who is supposed to have hit him. He had just recovered and regained his feet when Mr. Stroude came in, accused him of the crime and held him until we arrived.'

Burnett paused, and then went on: 'After I'd heard his story I searched for the letter he had been told to deliver, and of course,' he shrugged his shoulders, 'I didn't find it. The only thing that coincided in any way with his story was the lump on his head, and Mr. Stroude suggested a probable explanation for that.'

'How did he account for it?' asked Peter.

'Well,' replied the inspector, 'we neither of us believed this cock-and-bull story that Mason was trying to put across; it was too far-fetched altogether. The absence of the letter proved how absurd it was. If he had ever had it I should have found it on him, or somewhere in the room.'

'Unless the man who knocked him out, took it away with him?' suggested the reporter, and Burnett smiled indulgently.

'If there ever was such a person,' he answered sceptically. 'However, to revert to the bump on Mason's head. The floor by the window in the study is highly polished, and Stroude pointed out a long, scraped mark in the wax, such as would have been made if a man's foot had slipped. Close by there is a heavy oak table, and I don't think I'm very far wrong when I say that the bump on Mason's head was caused by him slipping on the shiny surface of the floor and striking his head against this table. It's a more likely explanation than his own, anyway.'

'H'm,' said Peter non-committally. 'Did you find any traces of the presence of this mysterious other man?'

'There were none,' said Burnett. 'The most convincing piece of evidence against Mason is the poker. I tested it for finger-prints and the only prints on it were his.'

'There were no others of any kind?' asked the reporter, raising his eyebrows.

'No.' Burnett gave a complacent smile.

'That certainly is strange,' said Peter thoughtfully. 'Supposing that Mason did kill Sir James,' he went on after a moment. 'What is your idea concerning his motive?'

'I don't think there's much doubt about that,' replied Burnett. 'Mason was out of a job, and penniless. He admits that he owes eight pounds to his landlady, and that she had threatened to turn him out. He came hoping to be able to pick up some money.'

'But he didn't know Sir James,' said Peter.

The inspector shrugged his shoulders eloquently. 'He *says* he didn't,' he replied.

'I'm sure he didn't,' said the reporter. 'Doesn't it strike you as strange that a penniless man should come all the way to High Wycombe at twelve o'clock at night, on the off chance of stealing, or in some way acquiring, money from a man he didn't know?'

'I don't know,' said Burnett. 'We're not definitely sure he didn't know him, and it's pretty well known that Sir James used to keep fairly large sums of money in the house.'

Peter made a grimace. 'Poor old Mason seems to be in anything but an enviable position,' he admitted. 'However, I don't believe he did it. One thing you've told me seems to point to his innocence.'

'Really?' Burnett's bushy eyebrows shot up in his surprise. 'What's that?'

'The finger-prints on the poker,' answered the reporter.

The inspector's mouth opened in an O of astonishment. 'But that's the biggest evidence against him,' he protested.

'It may be,' agreed Peter, 'and at the same time it may be the biggest evidence in his favour. It all depends.'

'Upon what?' asked the other.

'Upon whether there was a fire burning in the study grate on the night of the murder,' was the reply.

'There was,' answered Burnett, 'but I

don't see what that's got to do with it.'

'Don't you?' Peter smiled quietly. 'Well, I'm not going to explain now, but it's very simple.' He rose to his feet. 'Can I see Mason now?'

Burnett nodded, and led him through a door into the back of the station, and along a stone corridor from which the cells opened. Unlocking the middle one, he ushered the reporter into the presence of Dick Mason. The accused man was seated dejectedly on his pallet bed, but he rose at Peter's entrance and welcomed him eagerly.

'Betty was a brick to go and see you,' he cried, 'and it was awfully good of you to come along so promptly. Do you think there's any chance of getting me out of this ghastly mess?'

'I don't know, old man,' answered Peter, 'but I'm going to do my best. Now tell me all that you've already told the police, and anything else that you may have forgotten to tell them. I want to know exactly what happened on the night of the murder, and everything that led up to your going to Maddox Court.'

Without wasting time Dick plunged into his story, and the reporter listened attentively, but he learned very little more than he had already heard from Burnett.

'Did you see anything of this fellow who hit you?' he enquired when Dick had concluded.

The other shook his head. 'No, I just saw a vague shadow, that's all,' he answered. 'I think he was masked, but I wouldn't swear to it.'

'Was he already in the room or did he come from outside?' said Peter, but again Dick shook his head.

'I couldn't tell you that either,' he confessed ruefully. 'He may have come from outside, or he may have been hiding behind the curtains. I was too upset at what I found to notice.'

'One more question then,' said the reporter. 'This letter you were supposed to deliver, was it in your pocket when you entered through the window?'

'No,' answered Dick. 'It was in my hand. I took it out of my pocket before I pushed the window open.'

'I see.' Peter scratched his chin. 'And

when you picked up the poker what happened to the letter?'

'I don't know. I don't remember,' said Mason. 'I suppose I must have dropped it.'

There was a moment's silence and then abruptly Peter held out his hand. 'All right, keep your pecker up,' he said as the other gripped it. 'I suppose there's nothing else you can think of, that's likely to help?'

Dick thought for a little while, and then shook his head. 'No, I can't think of anything else,' he answered, and Peter with a cheery grin, left him.

'Well, what do you think now?' asked Burnett as they returned to the charge room.

'I think what I thought before,' replied the reporter. 'I think he's speaking the truth. And if that's so there's more in this murder than appears on the surface, for the evidence against him is too conclusive to be accidental.'

'What do you mean?' asked the inspector, looking at him questioningly.

'Simply this,' retorted Peter. 'If Mason

is not lying, then he has been cleverly 'framed'.'

Burnett stood stock still staring at him, with an expression of dawning under-standing. 'I never thought of that,' he muttered. 'H'm, if you're right then we've still got to find the murderer.'

'I'm sure we have,' replied Peter. 'Now do you think we could go up to Maddox Court?'

7

The House of Death

Even in the darkness and drizzle of that unpleasant night, Maddox Court showed pretensions to beauty. The drive between the winding avenue of chestnuts that stretched their leafless branches overhead was well gravelled, and the rambling bulk of the house, creeper-covered and mellow with age, loomed up against its background of trees, an epitaph to the past.

'They didn't build this in the last hundred years,' remarked Peter, as he brought his little car to a halt outside the main entrance. 'Nor in the last three hundred.'

'You're right there, Peter,' said Burnett. 'They say that Maddox Court was an old building when Oliver Cromwell burned down the east wing. It's a beautiful place; you ought to see it by daylight. Poor Sir James was very proud of his home.'

Peter said nothing. The drip, drip, of the rain, and the dusk of the coming night seemed to cast a shadow over the whole place. The house looked cold, cold with the chill of age and death. No light burned in any of the upstairs windows, and from the utter stillness it might have been a tomb. Burnett pulled at a wrought-iron bell pull and from somewhere within came the faint answering jangle of an old-fashioned bell. After a few seconds a light sprang up behind the stained-glass transom over the front door, and it was opened. An elderly man in the conventional dress of a butler appeared on the threshold, but behind him hovering in the background Peter made out the burly form of a uniformed policeman, and was conscious of the presence of the tragedy.

'Good evening, sir,' said the butler, his eyebrows going up in slight surprise. 'I didn't know you were coming back. I thought you had finished?'

'I'm never finished,' said the inspector. 'There's just one or two additional enquiries we want to make.'

'Come in, sir.' The old man stood aside and ushered them into the hall. 'You'll be wanting to see the study I suppose. I'll — '

'Who is that, Gilder?' A low, rather sweet voice called the question, and raising his eyes in the direction from which the voice had come, Peter saw halfway down the big staircase, one of the most beautiful girls he had ever seen in his life.

He was not a susceptible man, but at the sight of that slim figure with its sad white face, he caught his breath. She was small and slender, and her wide-set eyes regarding them enquiringly were the colour of wet turquoise. Her plain black sleeveless frock accentuated the creamy fairness of her skin, and the short ash-blonde hair that clung closely to the well-shaped head. Her small curved mouth was without lipstick to aid its redness, and the soft cheeks and rounded chin bore the faintest trace of powder. She wore no jewellery except a large pearl ring on the third finger of her right hand.

'Who is it, Gilder?' She repeated the

question as she began to descened the stairs.

The butler explained.

'I didn't know you were coming back, Inspector Burnett,' she said, coming up to them. 'I thought that — that was all over. Surely there is no doubt — ' She stopped and looked from one to the other enquiringly.

'There is always a doubt, Miss Maddox, until after the trial,' said the inspector. 'Although we may be morally certain ourselves, we have to collect a sufficient amount of proof to put before a jury.'

She nodded and the sadness in her eyes was replaced by an expression of puzzlement. 'But surely you have proof enough?' she said. 'There can't be any mistake, can there? Mr. Stroude found the man actually in the room.'

'All the same there are still a lot of details to be attended to,' said Burnett, 'and it's necessary for us to have another look round. I'm sorry to have to trouble you again at a time like this, but — '

'Oh, I don't mind, I don't mind at all,'

she said quickly. 'I'm only anxious that — that the person who did this terrible thing should be punished, who ever it was. Please go where you like, and do what you like, and if there's anything I can do to help, I will.'

'I don't think we shall have to trouble you, Miss Maddox,' said the inspector. 'But I may want to see Mr. Stroude again presently.'

'Gilder will tell him when you wish to see him,' she said. 'I shall be in the drawing-room if you want me, Gilder.' She bowed slightly to Burnett, and leaving the little group disappeared through a door on the left of the wide hall.

'You have the key of the study, sir,' said Gilder. 'You locked it, and took it away with you, if you remember.'

'That's right, I've got it here,' answered the inspector, crossing the hall to another door that almost faced the one through which the girl had gone.

'You won't want me, will you, sir?' asked the butler.

Burnett shook his head. 'Not for the

moment,' he answered. 'If I do there's a bell in the study that will bring you, isn't there?'

'Yes, sir,' said Gilder.

'Right, then I'll ring if I want you,' said the inspector, and the elderly man left them.

'Anything I can do, sir?' The constable who had been watching them came over to Burnett.

'No, I don't think so, Wipple,' said the inspector. 'Nothing to report, I suppose?'

'No, sir.'

Burnett took a key from his pocket, and stooping, unlocked the door of the fatal room. As Peter crossed the threshold he reached round and switched on the electric light.

The study was a pleasant room. It was difficult to believe that it had been the scene of a brutal murder, difficult until he saw the irregular dark stain that spread over the thick carpet. Wide french windows faced south and opened onto a gravel walk, bordered by a low hedge, beyond which could be seen a glimpse of the shaven lawn. Into a panel over the wide stone fireplace had been let the portrait by Van Dyck of that Maddox who had held the house for his king against the Puritans. His sombre eyes met Peter's, and it struck the reporter that accustomed as they may have been to scenes of bloodshed, they could have witnessed nothing grimmer than the tragedy that had been so recently enacted below his picture.

The furniture was old, good, substantial stuff, that is not turned out by modern workmen, working on the mass-production principle. In front of the fireplace was a deep leather armchair; other armchairs and a long settee stood against the bookshelves that covered the lower part of the wall. There were many books — the low cases were full of them — and as a room will often supply a key to the character of its owner, so this room gave Peter an insight into the habits of the dead man.

Order and neatness predominated. The surface of the large black-oak writing table in the centre was eloquent, with its clean blotting-paper, new nibs, heavy silver ink stand, without a spot of ink to mar its brightness, and the day-by-day calendar whose arrested record testified that this orderly activity had ceased for ever. Standing by the door, Peter took in every detail of the arrangement of the room.

'The place hasn't been touched, I suppose?' he said at length, and Burnett shook his head.

'No,' he replied, 'it's exactly as it was, except, of course, for the body. That's upstairs in his bedroom.'

The reporter crossed slowly over, and stood looking down at the uneven stain that clotted the pile of the carpet. 'Was he lying with his head towards the window, or how?' he asked.

'With his head towards the window,' answered the inspector.

'I see.' Peter nodded, and his eyes roved towards the writing table.

By the side of the spotless blotting pad, lay an open book. A chair with its back towards the window had been slewed half round.

The reporter came over to the writing

table, and looking down at the book, began idly to turn its pages. Suddenly he stopped, and bent lower.

'I see,' he said again under his breath.

'What do you see?' The interested Burnett was at his side in a moment, attracted by the change in his voice.

'The dead man was sitting here reading when the first blow was struck,' muttered Peter, his forehead wrinkled in thought. 'It dazed him but it didn't kill him, and he started up to grapple with his assailant. He staggered away from the table towards the window, and the last and final blow was struck — there.' He pointed to the dark patch on the carpet.

Burnett snorted disparagingly. 'What's all this Sherlock Holmes stuff?' he demanded. 'How do you know all that?'

'It's obvious by this,' Peter laid his hand lightly on the chair, 'and this.' He touched the open book. 'This book was open just now, but it was not open at the place he was reading when the murderer hit him. Half a dozen of the pages had sprung back. Look! Here is the place that it was *really* open at last night.'

Burnett looked and saw on the printed pages several spatters of dried blood. A shade of annoyance crossed his face. 'I never noticed that,' he confessed with a frown. 'Still, I don't see that it makes much difference where the first blow was struck.'

'It makes all the difference in the world,' said Peter, and his eyes were gleaming with suppressed excitement. 'It practically proves that Mason is innocent and the victim of a very clever plot.'

'Oh, come now, Peter,' protested the inspector. 'What's all this stuff you're trying to pull on me? How can — '

'Listen,' the reporter broke in, speaking rapidly. 'Imagine the scene last night when this murder was committed. Sir James is sitting here reading and Mason comes through the window. He comes in, let us say for the sake of argument, without making sufficient noise to disturb the man at the writing table. What does he do then?'

'He creeps up behind him and strikes,' said the inspector impatiently. 'That's simple enough.'

'Is it?' retorted Peter. 'What does he strike him with?'

'The poker — ' began Burnett and stopped, his mouth half open.

'Yes,' cried Peter quickly. 'Exactly — the poker which was over there in the fireplace *facing* Sir James, and which Mason could not possibly have got without walking *right across the room*.'

'Gosh!' breathed the inspector excitedly. 'I see what you're driving at.'

'It is ridiculous to suppose,' went on the reporter 'that Sir James would have continued to sit quietly reading while a perfect stranger came in by the window, walked over in front of his desk to the fireplace, picked up the poker, and came all the way back to hit him with it. I say it's absurd, and therefore it *didn't* happen.'

'Isn't it possible,' suggested Burnett, 'that Sir James had fallen asleep?'

'It's possible,' agreed Peter, 'but there again you're up against the evidence of the poker.'

'I don't quite see what you mean.' The inspector pursed his lips doubtfully.

'Those finger-prints,' explained the reporter. 'I told you that they first made me certain that Mason was speaking the truth.'

'I still don't see,' muttered Burnett, shaking his head.

'When you tested that poker, you found no other prints but Mason's,' explained Peter, 'and yet the poker was in use. I asked you if there was a fire in here on the night of the murder, and you said there was.'

'Good God! What a fool I am!' exclaimed Burnett, interrupting as the other's meaning dawned on him. 'Of course!'

'Oh, you see now, do you?' said Peter triumphantly. 'The poker must have been used many times during the day to stir the fire, either by Sir James himself, or one of the servants, and yet the only prints that showed were Mason's. It is inconceivable that there should not have been others. The only possible explanation is obvious. The poker had been carefully wiped clean, before the murder was committed.'

'In that case the murderer would have

left prints,' disagreed the Inspector.

'Not if he'd worn gloves,' said Peter, shaking his head, 'and, being a careful man, I'll bet that's what he did. I'm afraid you've got the wrong man, Burney. Mason's story is true.'

'Then who the dickens killed the old man?' demanded Burnett.

Peter shrugged his shoulders. 'That's still got to be found out,' he said. 'But I think we've got a good indication in which direction to look.'

'Have we?' muttered the inspector dubiously. 'I haven't noticed it!'

'I think it's pretty clear that the murderer was someone that Sir James knew,' said Peter. 'Someone he knew sufficiently well not to be disturbed when they came into the room while he was sitting reading. He knew the murderer so well that he did not bother to look up from his book. In other words, the person who killed him was either a great personal friend, whose appearance at such an hour would not surprise him, or' — he lowered his voice guardedly — 'some member of this household!'

8

The Mark on the Glass

Inspector Burnett looked at Peter for some seconds in silence.

'Well,' he said at length, expelling a long breath, 'I don't mind telling you that you've upset all my ideas pretty thoroughly, young feller. I didn't think there was the slightest chance of Mason's innocence, but now' — he shrugged his shoulders — 'well, I'm not so certain.'

'I'm glad you've changed your mind,' said Peter, smiling with satisfaction. 'This means you'll have to alter all your ideas, Burney, and start over again.'

The Inspector made a grimace. 'I'm afraid I shall,' he muttered. 'The question is, where to start.'

'I suggest you start by assuming that Mason's story is true in every detail,' said Peter, 'and then see if you can't find some trace of the man who struck him down, and who was either the murderer himself or someone working in collusion with the murderer.' He stopped and shot a quick glance at the worried Burnett. 'Look here,' he went on. 'I came into this partly to try and help Mason, but I shall be staying on behalf of the *Megaphone*. Suppose you let me work with you?'

The inspector's lips pursed, and he scratched his chin hesitantly. 'I don't know that I can do that, Peter,' he said dubiously. 'The regulations — '

'Hang the regulations!' broke in the reporter. 'I've helped you up to now, you must admit that. Come on,' he urged as he saw his friend weakening, 'stretch a point.'

'You'll have to promise not to print anything without my permission,' said Burnett, 'and you'll have to turn over everything you discover to the police. Do you agree to that?'

'I agree to that.' Peter nodded. 'It's on then?'

The inspector inclined his head reluctantly, although it was only at the thought of what his superiors might have to say regarding this unorthodox arrangement. For himself he rather welcomed the reporter's help. Peter was shrewd and had a reputation for nosing out the truth in the most difficult cases, and this looked as if it were going to be difficult enough, heaven knew.

'Let's have a look round, then, and see what we can find,' said Peter briskly. 'You haven't got a torch have you? These shaded lights don't show things up very well.'

Burnett shook his head. 'Wipple's got one, I think,' he said. 'Half a minute and I'll see.'

He went over to the door and called the constable, and a moment later came back carrying a powerful pocket lamp. Peter took it from him, and switching it on swept the light over the expanse of polished wood that separated the carpet from the french window. Carefully he went over the whole space, paying particular attention to the corners behind the swinging folds of the curtains. Presently with a little grunt of disappointment, he straightened up.

'There are plenty of marks,' he said, 'but none of them are clear enough to give us any useful information. It looks as though somebody might have been standing behind that left-hand curtain, but it's impossible to be sure. You examined the windows of course?'

'Yes,' answered the inspector. 'They were unlatched and hadn't been forced in any way.'

'Another point in Mason's favour,' muttered Peter. 'Last night was cold and wet and it is unlikely that Sir James would have been sitting here with the windows open.'

He went over and examined them carefully. 'This latch is one of those that can only be worked from the inside,' he said, 'so Mason couldn't possibly have opened it himself from outside. You see the more you look into this business, the more evident it becomes that he was the victim of a — Hallo, what's this?'

He bent forward, peering eagerly at one of the panes of glass.

'What have you found now?' asked Burnett.

'Something that I might easily have missed, and I'm sure you did,' answered Peter. 'The light of the lamp showed it up. Look here, on this glass! There's an impression of four fingers and a thumb. The marks that would be made by somebody resting their open hand against the pane outside while they leaned forward to peer into the room.'

'They're probably Mason's,' said the Inspector. Peter shook his head.

'I don't think they are,' he answered. 'The hand that made them was short and squat. Mason has rather long, thin hands.'

Burnett came over and peered at the marks. 'We ought to get them photographed,' he muttered. 'They may be an important clue. I'll send Wipple back to the station for a camera.'

While he was gone to give his orders to the constable, Peter opened the french window, and stepped out on to the gravel path beyond. He made a diligent search, but the rain had obliterated whatever traces there may have been, and after a little while he returned to the study. Burnett had sent the constable off on his errand, and returned, and to him Peter reported his failure at finding anything of interest outside.

'I wish you'd send for Stroude now,' he said. 'I'd like to hear what he has to say. And if you don't mind I'd like to ask him one or two questions myself.'

The inspector went over to the fireplace, and pressed the bell.

'I shan't mention who you are,' he said as they waited for an answer to his summons. 'That's the best way, I think. They might not like it if they thought you were a reporter.'

Peter nodded, and there came a tap on the door, and Gilder appeared.

'I should like to have a word with Mr. Stroude,' said Burnett in answer to the butler's enquiry. 'Would you kindly ask him to come here if he can spare a minute.'

'Yes, sir.' The old man nodded and withdrew.

The man who came in after a very short delay was tall and fair. At first glance he appeared to be about twenty-five, but when he advanced further into the room and the full light shone on his face, it was possible to distinguish the tiny lines round his mouth and eyes which the passing of many more years than those had stamped there. His complexion was fresh, almost florid, and there was a slight humorous twinkle in his deep-set eyes that was curiously cancelled by the thin line of his lips. Peter decided that Mr. Stroude was rather a complex character.

'You wish to see me?' he greeted them in a pleasant voice that possessed the faintest trace of a lisp.

'I'm sorry to have to trouble you again, Mr. Stroude,' said Inspector Burnett genially, 'but there are one or two extra questions that I should like to ask you.'

'No trouble at all,' replied the secretary. 'Only too pleased to do anything I can. Shocking affair.' He crossed leisurely over and sat down in a chair by the fireplace facing them. 'I can't get the sight of the poor old man out of my mind,' he said, shaking his head. 'I hope that fellow gets it hot and strong.'

'He'll get what he deserves, if he's

guilty,' said the inspector, and the other shot him a quick glance and raised his eyebrows.

'There's no question about that, is there?' he asked. 'Why, I found him bending over the body.'

'Every man is innocent until he is proved otherwise,' said Burnett rather sententiously. 'The evidence against this man Mason is very strong, but you will understand that it is our duty to substantiate every detail carefully before submitting our case to a jury.' He paused but Stroude looked at him silently, and waited. 'Now I want you to cast your mind back to yesterday evening,' he went on, 'say from the beginning of dinner. What time was that?'

'The usual time,' answered the secretary. 'Sir James was most particular regarding punctuality. We always dined at seven-thirty.'

'And you did so last night?'

'Yes.'

'What time did you finish?'

'Between half-past eight and a quarter to nine.'

'Was that your usual time for finishing dinner?'

'Yes, within a few minutes.'

'Who was present at the meal?' asked the inspector.

'Sir James, his daughter, Mr. Frank Lane, Sir James's nephew and myself.'

'Does Mr. Lane live here?'

'No.' Stroude settled himself more comfortably and crossed his legs. 'He has a flat in town. He motored down and motored back.'

'What time did he leave?'

'At about a quarter to eleven, I think. I can't be sure exactly as to the time. I was working on some accounts for Sir James in my own room.'

'Do you usually work in your own room?' It was Peter who asked the question this time, and the secretary turned his eyes in his direction and stared at him for a moment before he replied.

'No, I usually work in here,' he answered, 'but last night Sir James said he wanted to be alone as he was going to be busy.'

The reporter nodded. 'I see,' he said.

'He didn't say anything that suggested he wished to be alone because he was expecting someone?'

'No.'

'Had he any friends in the neighbourhood who were likely to call on him late at night?'

The secretary shook his head. 'Sir James had no intimate friends in the neighbourhood at all,' he replied. 'He had very few friends of any sort. He was rather a self-contained man, and preferred his own company.'

'I see,' said Peter again, and he looked across at Burnett with a glance that signified he had finished for the time being.

'Tell me, Mr. Stroude,' said the inspector, 'was Sir James his usual self last night?'

'I didn't notice any difference. He seemed the same at dinner.'

'And during the day?'

'Yes.'

'Exactly the same as usual?' put in Peter. 'He didn't appear to be worried about anything?'

'No, but that wouldn't necessarily mean that he wasn't,' answered Stroude. 'Sir James was the type of man who kept his feelings well under control.'

'What happened after dinner was over?' Peter went on after a slight pause, and Stroude wrinkled his brows in an effort to remember.

'Miss Maddox left us just after the port was served,' he said, 'and I believe went up to her own sitting-room to write some letters. That's what she said she was going to do. The rest of us sat smoking and talking for about twenty minutes, and then I left Sir James and his nephew together, and went to my room to get on with some work.'

'Did you go straight to your own room?'

'No, I came in here first to collect some papers that I wanted.'

'What time would that be?'

Stroude shook his head.

'I couldn't say for certain,' he answered. 'I should think somewhere about half-past nine.'

'Can you remember when you came in

here whether the windows were shut or open?'

'They were shut.'

'You are certain of that?'

'Absolutely.'

'Why are you so certain? Couldn't they just as easily have been not quite closed without your noticing?'

'No,' answered the secretary. 'While I was getting the papers I wanted, I heard a sound outside which I thought was rain, and went to the window to see. I remember quite clearly that they were shut and fastened.'

'And then you went to your room?'

'Yes.'

'And you remained there until — when?'

'Until I came down just after twelve, to bring my completed work to Sir James, and found him lying dead and that fellow bending over him.'

'How did you know, then, what time Sir James's nephew left?'

'I didn't know, until I asked Gilder.' The secretary looked from one to the other. 'May I enquire the object of all these questions?' he said. 'It seems to me since you've got the man, to be rather a waste of time.'

'Purely routine,' explained Inspector Burnett hastily. 'That's all, Mr. Stroude. We have to follow a certain set rule in these matters.'

'Red tape, eh?' said Stroude and smiled. 'Oh well, carry on.'

'Did you hear anything while you were working in your room?' asked Peter. 'A cry or the sound of a fall?'

'Nothing.'

'Where is your room?'

'On the first landing, almost immediately above this room.' The secretary gave an almost involuntary glance towards the ceiling.

'Then if Sir James had called for help, you would have heard him?'

'I might and I might not.' Stroude uncrossed his legs, and shifted his position. 'This house is very solidly built, and I was typing most of the time.'

'What were the relations between Sir James and his nephew?' asked Burnett. 'Friendly?'

'So far as I know,' was the reply.

'They always appeared on the best of terms. As I said before, Sir James was a man who hid his feelings. They might have been the bitterest enemies in the world in private, and no one would have known it.'

The inspector nodded and glanced at Peter, but the reporter was fiddling with a long penholder on the writing table, and evinced no desire to ask any further questions.

'I think that's all then, Mr. Stroude,' said Burnett. 'You understand that these questions I have been putting to you are purely a matter of routine. I don't think there will be any need to trouble you again until the inquest.'

Stroude rose. As he crossed to the door, Peter suddenly said casually: 'Oh, by the way, Mr. Stroude, do you happen to know the contents of Sir James' will?'

The secretary turned with his hand on the knob. 'I believe with the exception of a few bequests to servants, his entire property goes to his daughter,' he replied. 'His solicitors would know more about that than I.'

'Yes, of course,' said the reporter. 'Who are his solicitors?'

'Hake, Rand and Hake of Bedford Row,' answered Stroude.

'Thank you,' said Peter, and the secretary nodded and went out.

'That's a funny coincidence, if it *is* a coincidence,' muttered Peter almost to himself, and Burnett looked at him sharply.

'What's a funny coincidence?' he demanded.

'Mr. Hake of Hake, Rand and Hake has a private secretary called Betty Hardy,' answered the reporter. 'Betty Hardy is to all intents and purposes engaged to Dick Mason. Curious, isn't it?'

'H'm, it's funny certainly,' said the inspector. 'But I don't see that it can be anything more than a coincidence.'

'Perhaps not,' remarked Peter thoughtfully. 'But I distrust coincidences, that sort anyway. There's a brain at the back of this business, Burney, a jolly clever brain. I don't know what it's all leading to, or the motive behind this murder, but I've

105

got a hunch that it's only part of a gigantic scheme.'

Burnett opened his mouth to reply, but at that moment Gilder came softly into the room. 'Miss Maddox wishes me to ask you if you would like anything, sir,' said the butler gently.

'That's very kind of her, Mr. Gilder,' began the inspector, 'but I don't think — '

Crack!

A sharp staccato report, followed by the tinkling crash of breaking glass, drowned his words. Something hummed wickedly past Peter's head and struck the panelling above the fireplace with a thud. The reporter swung round towards the french windows. There was a jagged hole in one of the panes, and the splintered glass lay in sparkling fragments on the polished floor beneath.

'Good God!' gasped the startled Burnett. 'That was a pistol shot!'

'Yes and the bullet was meant for me,' said Peter grimly, and striding across to the windows he flung them open, and peered out into the darkness.

'For God's sake, be careful!' exclaimed

the inspector, but he had no cause for alarm. The mysterious shooter had gone.

There was no sound now from outside except the rustle of falling rain, and the soft moan of the rising wind.

9

Exit Mr. Sneath

Peter shut the windows and gripped Burnett by the arm.

'Find out where everybody was in the house at the time of that shot,' he whispered quickly.

The inspector nodded, and pushing past the frightened butler went out into the hall. As he emerged from the study the drawing-room door opened and Stroude appeared.

'What was that noise?' he asked sharply. 'It sounded like a shot.'

'It was a shot,' answered Burnett. 'Where were you when you heard it?'

'In here,' answered the secretary, nodding in the direction of the room he had just left. 'I was talking to Miss Maddox.'

As he spoke the slight figure of the girl appeared in the doorway.

'What was it? What has happened?' she asked in a frightened voice.

'Somebody shot at me through the study window,' said Peter before the inspector could reply. 'Mr. Stroude was in the drawing-room with you?'

'Yes.' She looked from one to the other with wide, scared eyes. 'We were talking when we heard the report and breaking glass.'

'And Gilder was in the study with us,' said the reporter quickly. 'How many other people are there in this house?'

'There's Wilkins, the footman, Dawson, Miss Maddox's maid, Baxter, the cook, the parlourmaid and two housemaids,' replied Stroude instantly.

'Is that all?' asked Burnett.

The secretary nodded. 'Yes, the gardeners and the chauffeur don't live in the house,' he said.

'Send for them all,' snapped the inspector.

Stroude gave an order to Gilder, and the old man hurried away.

'You don't think any of the servants would — would have done such a thing, do you?' said the girl in a low voice.

'I don't know,' answered Burnett. 'But I'd like to know where they all were.'

'But,' she protested, 'it's impossible that a member of the household — '

'Nothing is impossible, Miss Maddox,' interrupted Peter quietly. 'Of course, if everybody can give an account of their movements at the time that shot was fired, and prove that they're speaking the truth, then we shall know that we have to look for someone outside. Someone who is not a member of the household.'

'Why should you imagine that anyone in the house would fire at you?' asked Stroude.

'Because,' answered Peter coolly, 'I think somebody thought I might discover too much. That was the motive behind that bullet. And it's stretching one's credulity too far to suppose that the murderer of Sir James has been hanging about in the vicinity since he committed the crime for the purpose of trying to put me out of the running. The only logical conclusion, therefore, is that he was on the premises when I arrived.'

'But I don't understand.' the girl stared at him in astonishment. 'I thought you had got Daddy's — murderer.' She hesitated before the ugly word got past her lips.

'There is a possibility that he may have had an accomplice among the household,' said the reporter, and he fervently hoped that this obviously ridiculous theory would be accepted without question.

Apparently it was, or more likely there was no time for Stroude or the girl to argue over it, for Gilder came back at that moment shepherding the little flock of servants. They looked scared, and clung together in a frightened group. Burnett had them sent into the study one by one, and questioned each separately, but the total result yielded nothing. The footman and the cook had been in the kitchen and supplied each other with an alibi. They had heard the sound of the shot faintly, but had thought that it was a door being slammed. Dawson, the maid, had been trying on a dress that her mistress had given her, and the parlour-maid had been present to give her admiring approval.

The two housemaids had been upstairs at the top of the house sorting out some linen to go to the laundry. They had been in the other wing, and had not even heard the sound of the explosion. Neither Peter nor the inspector could find any loophole in these stories, and eventually dismissed the servants and sent them back to their duties.

'Miss Maddox supplies your alibi, Mr. Stroude,' said Burnett, 'and you supply hers, so there's nothing for it but to conclude that the shooter was someone outside of the household.'

He went outside and with Peter's help made a search of the gravel path, but he found nothing. The mysterious visitor had left no traces whatever. By the time they returned to the study, the constable had come back with the camera. The inspector made four careful exposures of the mark on the glass, repacked the camera and gave it to Wipple.

'Take that back to the station and give it to Sergeant Hare,' he ordered. 'Get him to knock up Ogden's, the chemist, and ask them to develop the plates at once and make half a dozen rough prints. Tell him to take them up to Scotland Yard right away. If they've got anything like them in records, he's to 'phone me here. Have you got that clear?'

The constable assured him that he had it quite clear, and took his departure. When he had gone, Peter and Burnett went in search of the dead man's daughter. They found her in the drawing-room sitting alone and staring into the fire. Stroude had apparently gone up to his own room to work. She welcomed them with an attempt at a smile, but shook her sleek head when she heard what it was they wanted.

'I'm afraid I can't help you,' she said. 'So far as I know there was nothing in Daddy's life to account for this crime, and I'm sure I should have heard of it if there had been. Although he was always very reticent with other people, he always told me everything.' The tears gathered in her eyes, but she brushed them aside.

'On what kind of terms was Mr. Frank Lane with his uncle?' asked the inspector, putting the same question he had previously put to Stroude.

'They were quite friendly,' she answered. 'He used to come and dine here once a month.'

'As far as you know,' continued Burnett, 'there was nothing in the nature of bad blood between them?'

'No.' She seemed rather surprised at the question. 'Of course, their tastes were totally dissimilar. Mr. Lane has a private income that was left him by an aunt, and he's inclined to be, well, a little extravagant. I've often heard Father arguing with him about that, and saying that it was a pity he couldn't find something to occupy his time. But it was quite in a friendly way.'

'Oh, Mr. Lane has a private income of his own, has he?' said Peter, speaking for the first time.

'Yes, quite a large one, I believe,' she replied.

'What other relations have you besides Mr. Lane?' asked the reporter.

She glanced at him rather curiously and hesitated.

'There's Mr. Lane's brother, John,' she

114

said at last, reluctantly, 'but — ' She stopped abruptly.

'But what?' prompted Peter gently.

'Well, we — we never mention him,' she went on, as though the information were being dragged from her against her will. 'He's rather — the — black sheep of the family, if you understand what I mean?'

Peter pricked up his ears. Here was information that might be of importance.

'In what way?' he asked. 'I don't want to probe into family secrets, Miss Maddox, but you must realise that in a case like this it is necessary.'

'Oh yes, I do,' she answered, but her troubled expression deepened and she twisted her ring nervously on her finger. 'But I don't think John could have had any connection with — with Daddy's death. You see, he hasn't seen him or been near the house for over three years. Not since they — they quarrelled.'

'You mean he and your father?' said the reporter.

She nodded.

'What was the quarrel about?' he asked.

'I believe it was over money,' she replied. 'John had got himself into the hands of some moneylenders and wanted Father to help him, but Father refused. He had helped him several times before but John is one of those people whom you could help over and over again without doing any permanent good. Father said that if he got him out of this trouble, he would only get into some more, and that as long as somebody would keep on helping him, he would never try to help himself. There was a dreadful scene, I remember. John accused Father of all sorts of things, and eventually Father lost his temper and ordered him out of the house. Since then we've never heard anything of him.'

Inspector Burnett, who had listened to this recital with interest, looked up quickly as she stopped. 'Where does this Mr. John Lane live?' he asked.

She shook her head. 'That I don't know,' she replied. 'Possibly father's solicitors would know. I believe an arrangement was made to pay him a small weekly allowance, and as it was paid by them they are bound to know his address.'

Peter made a mental note to try and obtain this information from Messrs. Hake, Rand and Hake at the first opportunity. John Lane was distinctly worth enquiring into. It would be interesting to know exactly where he had been on the night, and at the time, that the murder had been committed. Up to the present he seemed to fit the requirements of the murderer. He was well known to Sir James and his appearance at that hour would not have aroused the elder man's suspicion, particularly if there had been some sort of an appointment made. Peter concluded that John Lane was most certainly worth following up.

He began to chat cheerfully to the girl, slipping in an unobtrusive question here and there, and Burnett dropped out of the conversation altogether and sat listening in silence. But the net result that he learned was meagre. At least he thought so at the time, though it was destined to have a direct bearing on the mystery, and eventually lead him to the truth.

Margaret Maddox was twenty, her next birthday falling on the second of the following month. Her mother had died at her birth, and her father, who was in India, had arrived home to find a motherless child barely six weeks old. She had been brought up by a nurse, a woman named Berman, who was now living on a small pension given her by Sir James. Margaret and her father had apparently been the closest of friends, and the gap in her life left by his sudden and dreadful death would take a long time to fill. This was the sum total of what Peter succeeded in gently extracting from her, and at the time he could see nothing in it that was likely to help. Presently Stroude joined them, and a little later Burnett and the reporter went back to the study. They were eating sandwiches and drinking hot coffee when Gilder came in to say that Burnett was wanted on the 'phone. The instrument was in the hall and the Inspector was gone for some time.

When he came back his face betrayed his excitement.

'That was the Yard,' he said. 'They've found a record of those prints in R.O.'

'Whose are they?' asked Peter quickly.

'A man called William Sneath,' answered Burnett. 'He appears to have done a bit of everything, from 'whizzing' to burglary. He's also a 'nose' in his spare time. They say he's the fellow who shopped Rosenthal, the fence, and Abe Guiness, the smash-and-grabber.'

'That looks like our man,' said Peter. 'Anyway he was certainly here on the night of the murder. If he didn't actually kill Sir James himself, I'm pretty sure he knows all about it. He shouldn't be difficult to get hold of. What do you say to going up to town to see if we can find him?'

Burnett was agreeable to this, and Peter put a call through to his friend Mr. Trimmer. A few seconds later they had left Maddox Court and were on their way to London. It was nearly eleven o'clock when they wearily climbed the stone stairs to Chief-Inspector Trimmer's cheerless office.

Mr. Trimmer greeted Peter with his usual lazy grunt.

'Come in,' he said sleepily. 'If you sit on the desk, Inspector Burnett can have that chair.'

'We're not stopping,' said Peter quickly. 'All we've come for is this man Sneath's address.'

'I'll get it for you.' The melancholy inspector stretched out a lean hand and pressed a bell.

To the constable who came in answer to the summons he gave an order, and while they waited for the man's return he chatted to Burnett. 'I suppose you won't be calling us in?' he said sadly.

The inspector smiled and shook his head. 'Not if I can help it,' he replied.

'Thought you wouldn't,' murmured Mr. Trimmer, helping himself to one of his eternal Woodbines. 'Well, I hope you manage the affair all right by yourself. That's the trouble with you local fellers. You try to do things on your own, an' when you fall down you call on us to help you, an' expect us to do miracles, although by the time we get into the case it's ancient history, an' all the clues have been messed up.' He sighed wearily. 'What are you doin' in this business?' he looked across at Peter.

'Everything!' said the reporter immodestly.

'H'm! Well between you,' remarked Mr. Trimmer shaking his head, 'there ought to be a very good chance of the murderer gettin' away.'

The constable came back at that moment with a folder which he laid on the desk, and withdrew. The lugubrious inspector flipped it open, and frowned down at it.

'Rose Water Lane, Battersea,' he said. 'That's where he lives. Number six. An' if you're expectin' green fields and meadows, an' ripplin' streams, you're going to get a shock.'

'Is he the sort of man who would commit a murder?' added Burnett, and Mr. Trimmer shrugged his shoulders.

'Any sort of man would commit a murder if the motive was strong enough,' he replied cynically. 'But the motive would have to be darned strong in Sneath's case.

He might if he was very desperate, and driven into a corner. But otherwise I don't think he's got the nerve.'

'You don't think he's capable of planning a deliberate crime?' said Peter.

The inspector shook his head contemptuously. 'Not murder,' he said. 'He'd plan blackmail, or bustin' a shop or anythin' like that, but he's too scared of his precious skin to go in for a killin'.'

'Thanks, that's all we want to know.' Peter was at the door in two quick strides. 'Come on, Burney.'

'You're in a mighty hurry,' growled Mr. Trimmer. 'What — '

'We've got work to do,' answered the reporter, and he hurried down the stairs with Burnett at his heels.

He got into his little car which was waiting outside the entrance to the Yard, and when the inspector had taken his place beside him, sent it speeding in the direction of Battersea.

Rose Water Lane was even worse than he expected, and it took nearly ten minutes before they could make anybody hear at number six. After repeated knockings at the crazy door, however, a red-faced woman in a dirty flannel dressing gown appeared and glared at them malignantly.

'Wot cher want?' she demanded. 'Wakin' people at this time o' night. I was abed and asleep.'

A strong smell of gin wafted out as she spoke, which probably accounted not a little for her bad temper.

'You have a man living here named Sneath — ' began the reporter.

'Are you the police?' she demanded less truculently, and the question was anything but a recommendation to Mr. Sneath's character.

'I'm not connected with the police,' replied Peter truthfully, 'but I should like to see Mr. Sneath for a few minutes.'

'Why don't you call at respectable hours?' grumbled the woman. 'I'll tell 'im you're 'ere. 'oo shall I say?'

'Just say Mr. Escott would like to see him,' said Peter.

The woman departed into the dark interior and would have shut the door, only the reporter deftly inserted a foot.

They heard her laboriously mount the stairs, calling out to Sneath at intervals. Then there was a short silence, followed by a loud hammering on a door. The hammering was repeated and the woman muttered something about 'making enough noise to wake the dead.' There came the sound of a door opening and shutting, and then after a pause the heavy tread of the woman as she came back down the stairs.

'Ye'll 'ave to come again to-morrow,' she announced. ''e ain't in.'

'Not in?' said Peter. 'Does he usually stay out as late as this?'

''e usually comes in when 'e likes,' she snapped. 'I ain't 'is keeper, and 'e ain't in!'

She slammed the door, for Peter had withdrawn his foot at her approach and the reporter looked at Burnett.

'That's that!' grunted the inspector. 'It looks to me as if are too late, and Sneath has already made a getaway.'

'It does,' agreed Peter. 'What do we do now?'

'Go back to the Yard,' said the

inspector, 'and have an 'all stations' call sent out to pull him in.'

But this was unnecessary, for when they reached the Yard, Mr. Trimmer was full of information.

'I'm afraid you'll have me in on this case after all,' he said dolefully. 'We've just had a call from the police station at Putney. The body of a man was discovered an hour ago on the edge of the common.'

'What's that got to do with us?' demanded Peter.

'Everythin',' replied Mr. Trimmer. 'The dead man was William Sneath!'

10

A Visit to Mr. Hake

The divisional surgeon was making his report when Peter, Inspector Trimmer and Burnett reached the place where the dead man had been discovered.

'He was shot at close range by a very small bore pistol,' was the doctor's verdict. 'He's been dead about three hours I should say.'

Near to the body was an empty taxi cab. It had been pulled in to the side of the road and left with its lights burning, and it was this that had first drawn the attention of the patrolling policeman who had discovered the crime to the body a few yards away. A search of the dead man's pockets revealed nothing. Any papers he might have been carrying had been taken by the murderer. After the usual photographs had been taken, and Inspector Trimmer had made a brief examination of the scene of the crime, an ambulance was sent for and all that was mortal of Mr. William Sneath was taken away to the mortuary. A constable started up the engine of the taxi, and drove it into the yard attached to the police station for closer inspection, Peter following in his own car with Burnett. There was no doubt that the man had been shot in the cab. There was a bullet hole through the leather lining of the hood.

'The murderer fired twice, that's obvious,' said Mr. Trimmer gloomily. 'There's a second bullet imbedded in the floor board. The driver of the cab is the man we want, though I don't suppose it's going to be easy to find him.'

His pessimism was unjustified, for he was found very speedily.

His name was Coop, and as well as being the driver he was also the owner of the taxi. He proved to be a very thin and very alarmed man. His story was a simple one, and there seemed no reason to doubt its truth. He had got to the garage where he usually left his cab a little before eight o'clock. It was a private lock-up garage, situated in a small yard near Southampton Row. When he reached it, he found that he had left his key at home. He had been out very early that morning, and he lived a good way away and was very tired. He left the cab outside the door in the yard. He had, he said, left it once or twice before without any trouble when he had forgotten his key. He thought it would be perfectly safe because cabs are very rarely stolen. They are useless to the average car thief, because they are so easily identified, and for this reason the 'knocker off' usually leaves them severely alone. So far as Mr. Coop was concerned, he had a complete alibi, for he had gone to the nearest police station after leaving the cab, to deposit an umbrella and a pair of gloves left behind by a previous fare, and from there straight home. The stable yard where his garage was situated was quite a lonely place, and unlike the majority was entirely without inhabitants, the garage being part of a building which was used as a furniture store.

There was nothing further to be learned from the cab, or its scared driver, and Peter, after a few words with Inspector Trimmer and Burnett, took his leave. He had had a long day and he was feeling very tired, but there was still a lot for him to do before he could go to bed.

He drove from Putney to the offices of the *Megaphone* and by the time he reached that palatial building, he had decided on the form his story would take. He typed and turned in his 'copy' to the night editor, and the story that the *Megaphone* printed on the following morning was substantially the same as that carried by every other newspaper.

It was getting on for two when he reached his flat, but even then he did not go to bed. With a cigarette between his lips he sat down in front of the gas fire in the sitting-room and thought.

Betty Hardy had introduced him to a case that was as puzzling as any in his experience. This was no ordinary crime with a clear motive. There was at present no motive visible at all. What connection was there between the murder of Sir James Maddox and the little nose, William Sneath? Why had Sneath been killed too? Had he seen too much that night at Maddox Court, when he had left the impression of his hand pressed against the window? Had he seen the old man struck down, seen the face of the murderer and so rendered his further existence a menace to the killer's safety? Or had he been in the plot and tried to make a little on the side by his usual trick of blackmail? The latter seemed the most likely. It was difficult otherwise to account for his presence at Maddox Court at all, but then it was difficult to account for anything in this extraordinary mix-up. Why had Sir James been killed, and who had planned and carried out the murder so carefully, cleverly arranging to involve Mason in the crime? Was the man responsible the black-sheep nephew, John Lane, and if so what was his motive? That seemed to Peter to be the starting link in the whole chain. Without that there was no jumping-off place. The motive must be a very strong one, but what was it? Gain? Vengeance? Or self-preservation? Had Sir James known something about somebody that made it essential for him to be silenced, or had he done something that engendered such a hatred that only his death could satisfy? Or lastly, did his death entail the enriching of some hitherto unknown person? The will would clear up this point. It would also show how much John Lane stood to gain by his uncle's death. Peter rose at last and stretched himself with a yawn. He must be about early on the following morning, or rather that morning, for there was a lot to be done.

He was up at seven, and his first call was at the tea-shop where Mason had stated he had had his interview with the man of the letter. He found the girl who had served them, but she could not remember what they were like. She recollected vaguely the two men coming in, but her description was indefinite. It could easily have applied to anybody. She couldn't even describe Dick Mason, beyond that 'he was youngish, you know.'

Peter gave it up, and proceeded from the tea-shop to Bedford Row. He arrived at the offices of Messrs. Hake, Rand & Hake just as Betty Hardy was taking off her coat and preparing for the day's work. She greeted him with a smile of pleasure, in which expectation and fear were curiously mingled.

'Mr. Hake hasn't arrived yet,' she said in answer to his first question. 'I don't suppose that he'll be long though. Did you see Dick?'

He told her all that had happened.

'I think you've done wonders,' she said gratefully. 'Do you think they'll release him now?'

'Not as quickly as that,' he answered. 'But I don't think you've got anything to worry about. But the way,' he added, 'did you know that this firm acted for Sir James Maddox?' She nodded.

'Yes,' she replied, 'but I didn't know it when I came round to see you.'

Peter looked surprised. 'But you're Mr. Hake's private secretary, aren't you?' he said.

'Yes, but there are one or two special clients whose affairs he never discusses with me, and whom I know nothing about,' she answered. 'Sir James was evidently one of these.'

'I see,' said Peter. 'Well, it's because Mr. Hake acted for Sir James that I want to see him. I'm hoping — '

A buzzer rang above the desk in the little office in which they were standing, and the girl picked up a pencil and pad.

'That's Mr. Hake,' she said. 'He must have come in while we were talking.'

Peter stooped to a little deception. A reporter is scrupulously honest unless he is working on a crime story, and then he is prepared to go to any lengths to obtain the information he requires. Peter had in his pocket a card which had been given him on a distant occasion by Mr. Trimmer. It was fairly clean, and it had that gentleman's name and rank together with an imposing 'New Scotland Yard' neatly engraved on its surface.

'Listen,' he leaned towards the girl and whispered. 'I don't want to interview Mr. Hake in my own capacity. Take this card and ask him if he can spare me a few minutes.'

What he was doing was thoroughly illegal, and he knew it. If the deception

133

was discovered he would get into serious trouble, but the risk never bothered him. Peter thrived on risks. The girl looked at the card and frowned.

'I don't like — ' she began but he over-ruled her scruples, and she passed through a communicating door into an inner office. After a lapse of less than half a minute she re-appeared.

'Mr. Hake will see you now,' she said and held open the door for the reporter to pass through.

He found himself in a private office, furnished more luxuriously than the average lawyer's, and in the presence of a huge man who was seated on the other side of a large flat-topped writing table, and seemed to dwarf it by his enormous size.

'Good morning — er — Chief Inspector.' The lawyer spoke in rather a nasal voice as though he suffered from adenoids. 'Sit down.' He waved a fleshy hand. 'Of course I know what you've come to see me about.'

'Then I needn't waste time in explanation,' replied Peter. 'I want to ask you a few questions regarding Sir James Maddox.'

'The late Sir James Maddox,' said Mr. Hake, slightly stressing the word 'late,' 'was a client of mine, and I do not discuss my client's affairs.'

'I quite understand that,' said the reporter, 'but in this case — '

'I can see nothing in this case to make me break the habit of a lifetime,' broke in the lawyer ponderously.

Peter's lips compressed. He knew the type of man he was dealing with. A man evidently bound up by tradition and red tape.

'It is unnecessary for me to point out,' he said quickly, 'that your client did not die a natural death, and therefore — '

'My client was murdered,' said Mr. Hake, nodding his large head. 'I am quite aware of that. I am also aware that the man who killed him is now in the hands of the police.'

'We are not quite certain of that,' said the reporter. 'That is the reason why I have come to see you.'

Mr. Hake's eyes suddenly became very

large. 'I don't understand you,' he said after an appreciable pause. 'Surely there can be no question regarding this man's guilt. He was found, so I have been given to understand, by the side of the body and his fingerprints were on the weapon with which the crime was perpetrated.'

'All the same, we're still rather doubtful,' said Peter, 'and although I respect your very natural disinclination to discuss your late client's private affairs, I am equally sure that you do not in any way wish to hamper the police in the discovery of the truth.' He thought privately that this was rather a good speech.

'That is perfectly true,' agreed the lawyer.

'Then perhaps you wouldn't mind telling me,' Peter went on, 'anything you may know concerning Sir James that will help us to clear up the mystery surrounding his death.'

Mr. Hake pursed his lips, and his fat hands played with an ivory paper knife that lay on the table before him. 'I know of nothing concerning Sir James' life that would in any way account for this murder,' he said after a pause. 'Nothing at all.'

'I suppose he made a will?' said Peter, and the other nodded.

'Yes,' he answered, 'his will was drawn up several years ago.'

'And who benefits by his death?' asked the reporter.

Mr. Hake hesitated. 'Since the contents of the will are likely shortly to become public property,' he answered after a little consideration, 'there is no reason why you should not know. With the exception of various bequests to servants and dependants, the whole of his estate, amounting to close on three-quarters of a million, goes to his daughter.'

Peter was staggered. 'I'd no idea such a large sum was involved,' he said.

'Sir James was a very rich man,' murmured Mr. Hake almost devoutly.

'And these bequests you spoke about, who benefits by them?' asked Peter.

'Several people,' replied the lawyer. 'I, myself, have been left two thousand pounds; Gilder, the butler who has been with the family nearly forty years, gets one thousand. Sir James's two nephews, Mr. Frank Lane and Mr. John Lane, each receive five thousand pounds, and there are one or two smaller sums to the chauffeur and other servants amounting in all to about five hundred pounds.'

'I see,' said the reporter. 'About this nephew of Sir James's, Mr. John Lane, from what I can gather from Miss Maddox he's rather a black sheep?'

Mr. Hake frowned slightly and hesitated. 'Well — er — yes in a way,' he admitted reluctantly. 'I believe he is rather wild and unbalanced. I don't think there's any particular harm in him. His trouble is mostly laziness and a complete lack of business ability.'

'There was some trouble between him and Sir James, wasn't there?' asked Peter.

The solicitor nodded. 'I'm afraid there was,' he said. 'Sir James and John Lane did not see eye to eye at all. My late client had views about life that were directly opposite to those of his young nephew.'

'Wasn't there some question of debts?' asked the reporter.

'There was a large question of debts,' said Mr. Hake. 'There was also rather an unpleasant affair with a moneylender that put the finishing touch. After that, Sir James, who had been very generous, refused to have anything more to do with his nephew, beyond arranging that I should pay him a small weekly allowance.'

'I take it,' said Peter, 'that there is a great difference between the two brothers.'

'Between Frank and John?' said Mr. Hake. 'Yes, there is a great difference. Frank is directly opposite in every way to his brother, but then of course he is much older. There is nearly fifteen years' difference between them, and he is also fairly well off. When his aunt died she left him a considerable sum.'

'And nothing to the younger brother?' enquired the reporter.

'A small amount only,' answered the solicitor. 'Two hundred and fifty pounds to be exact. I think this lasted John Lane about a week. She disapproved of his mode of living almost as much as Sir James.'

'What is Mr. John Lane's address?' said Peter after a little pause, and the solicitor looked at him keenly.

'What are all these questions leading to, Inspector?' he asked. 'Surely, there is no idea of suspecting either Frank or John Lane of having murdered their uncle?'

'No, no,' answered Peter, trying to assume an official expression. 'But in a case like this we have to seek for the motive. That is our weak point at present. From what you've told me it would seem that Sir James's death would benefit John Lane most. Five thousand pounds is not a large sum, but to a man who is being worried by moneylenders and others, a fortune.'

A troubled expression crossed the solicitor's big face. 'I can hardly believe,' he said, 'that John Lane would have taken such a terrible step to get out of any trouble he may have been in.'

'I'm not saying he did,' said the reporter, 'and if he can account for his movements on the night and at the time the crime was committed, that will be enough for us. But I'm afraid we shall have to see him and, therefore, I must ask you for his address.'

The solicitor pulled gently at a little hanging fold of flesh beneath his fat chin. 'I suppose in that case I'd better give it to you,' he said ungraciously.

He unlocked a drawer in his writing table, and took out a small book, bound in black leather. Flicking over the pages with his large forefinger, he presently stopped, consulted an item and looked across at the reporter.

'The address is Flat 7, Bently Buildings, Kilburn,' he said, and returning the book to the drawer, locked it.

'I'll make a note of that,' said Peter, and producing his pocket-book and pencil wrote it down.

He was going on to say something further, when a confused noise in the outer office stopped him. A woman's voice, rough and uncultured, was raised in anger.

'I don't care if the King's with 'im!' came the shrill tone, slightly muffled by the intervening door. 'I'm going to see 'im, an' I don't want none o' your sauce, see? Who are you, I'd like to know? The daughter of a man what was 'ung, that's what you are!'

'At the present moment I'm Mr. Hake's private secretary,' replied the voice of Betty. 'And I tell you that he's engaged. If you will wait — '

'D'ye think I've got nothing better to do, than 'ang round a mouthpiece's office?' replied the other angrily. 'You get away from the door, my girl; I'm going to see the old devil now!'

Mr. Hake uttered a smothered exclamation, and glancing across at him Peter saw with surprise that his fat face had gone a dirty shade of grey!

11

A Drunken Woman

The lawyer's heavy jaw dropped, and he was staring at the closed door with a hint of fear in his eyes. Catching Peter's glance, he pulled himself together with a supreme effort and coughed.

'I'm afraid — ' he began, but got no further, for his words were drowned by the noise of the door being flung violently open, and he gazed helplessly at the woman who stood on the threshold.

And so did Peter, unable to hide the astonishment in his eyes at this extraordinary apparition. She was very tall and gaunt, with large bony hands that were as big as a man's, and in one of which was clasped a very badly rolled umbrella. Her flat horse-like face was red and blotchy, and the thin nose jutted out arrogantly from between small and bead-like eyes that were set very close on either side of the high bridge. She was dressed in a tailor-made costume of a very loud check tweed, that was so creased and stained that it looked as though she had slept in it for over a week, and she was, as Peter saw at once, rather drunk.

'What d'ye mean by getting that chit to try and keep me out, Hake?' she demanded angrily and not altogether clearly. 'Ain't I got a right to come and see you when I want to? Ain't I of more importance than all your other 'igh falutin' clients put together? Ain't I?'

She glared ferociously at Peter.

'Who's this feller, anyway? Send him away, d'ye 'ear! I don't like 'im!'

'My dear lady,' said Mr. Hake soothingly, but she refused to listen.

'Oh, cut the cackle!' she snapped. 'Send 'im away, I tell you. I've got a lot to say to you.'

The lawyer's lips tightened.

'I really must ask you to wait, Mrs. Berman,' he remonstrated. 'I am engaged with this gentleman for a few minutes. If you will take a seat in the outer office — '

'I'm takin' no seat nowhere!' she broke

in. 'I came 'ere to see you, and see you I'm goin' to and at once! Tell this feller to come back later on.' She turned to Peter with a suppressed hiccough. ''ere you! 'Op it!' she said, jerking her thumb in the direction of the door. 'You ain't wanted, see? Run away and play!'

'Really I cannot allow this.' Mr. Hake rose, his face flushed with anger, and crossing the room whispered something in her ear.

Her ruddy colour faded and she went almost pale. Her watery eyes flashed a frightened glance at Peter, and her loose lips moved as though she were trying to speak.

'I'm sorry,' she muttered thickly. 'I didn't mean no 'arm, mister. Only I've got some partic'lar private business to talk over with my s'licitor. But don't mind me, I'll wait. I didn't know you was busy.'

She would have withdrawn, a cowed figure after her previous bluster, but the reporter also rose and turned to Hake.

'I don't think I need detain you any further,' he said pleasantly, 'I think I'll be getting along.'

145

He noted the look of relief that spread over the large face of the lawyer.

'I'm sorry I couldn't help you more than I have,' said Hake. 'If I should come across anything amongst Sir James's papers, I will get in touch with you at once.'

He shepherded Peter into the other office, and past the white-faced girl.

'I must apologise for that little scene in there,' he muttered, 'but Mrs. Berman is a very old client, and — er — well — er — between you and me not quite — ' He touched his forehead and smiled.

'Mrs. Berman?' Peter wrinkled his brows. 'Let me see, wasn't she Miss Maddox's nurse at one time?'

'Yes.' Mr. Hake was rather startled at his knowledge. 'She receives, or rather, she did receive, a pension from Sir James. I am more indulgent to her than I should be on that account, and of course, because of her — er — slight mental derangement.'

'Her mental derangement seems to be caused by gin more than anything else,' remarked Peter dryly. 'Good-bye, Mr. Hake.'

He gripped the other's huge hand which felt rather like a dead codfish, and left the office. Halfway down the stairs he heard his name called softly, and looking round saw that Betty had followed him.

'Peter, did you hear what that dreadful woman said?' asked the girl breathlessly as she came up to him.

'I heard her say a lot of things,' replied Peter with a grin. 'Which particular thing are you talking about?'

'About me,' said Betty. 'About my being the daughter of a — of a man who had been hanged.'

'Yes I heard that.' Peter nodded.

She looked at him with troubled eyes. 'It can't be true,' she whispered, 'and yet it sounded as if she knew. But it can't be true, surely.'

'Don't you know whether it's true or not?' asked the reporter in surprise.

'No,' she answered, shaking her head. 'You see I never knew my father or my mother. They both died when I was a baby. I was brought up by my aunt, and when she died, I was about eighteen then and had been earning my own living for about three years, I went to live on my own.'

Peter scratched his chin. 'I can't remember the execution of anyone named Hardy,' he said thoughtfully. 'Have you ever seen this woman Berman before?'

'Oh yes, several times,' answered Betty. 'She comes here regularly once a month, but she never spoke to me before. She was always rather subdued.'

'Did you ever see Sir James?' asked the reporter.

'No,' she answered. 'As I told you I'd no idea that he was a client of Mr. Hake's.'

Peter walked back towards his flat rather thoughtfully. There was some mystery connecting the woman Berman with the lawyer. It looked as though she had some hold on the man — he remembered the half-frightened expression in Hake's eyes at the sound of her voice — and she had been in the employment of Sir James Maddox. Did the clue he was seeking lie in the hands of this drunken woman who apparently had the power to twist the dead man's solicitor round her finger? At least there was something abnormal here that would repay looking into. Peter felt that he had no reason to be dissatisfied with his morning's work. He had obtained the address of John Lane, and accidentally come upon something else that might prove to be a great help: The ungainly and unprepossessing Mrs. Berman.

By the time he reached his flat, he had come to the conclusion that Mrs. Berman, the stout lawyer and John Lane would all three be worth very close attention. He decided to take John Lane first.

At the exact moment that he reached this decision, Mr. Hake, with both doors of his office locked, was engaged in an urgent telephone conversation.

'She is trying blackmail,' he said, speaking in a low voice. 'That's all it amounts to, and I don't see exactly what we can do. She practically holds us in the hollow of her hand. One word from her and we should find ourselves in the dock.'

There was a pause, and then the voice at the other end of the wire replied.

'Then she mustn't be allowed to speak that word,' it said. 'Precautions must be taken at once. It shouldn't be difficult to silence her.'

The stout lawyer felt the perspiration spring out on his large face. 'You're not suggesting, that — ' he whispered huskily, and then: 'I won't be connected with any more of that! I haven't got over the other. I daren't sleep for fear of seeing him in my dreams.'

'It's the only way,' was the reply, 'unless you prefer fifteen years in prison! I think that's what you'd get. You're in this up to your neck, Hake, and you've got to go through with it! If Berman is proving troublesome she must be got rid of!' There was a slight pause and then the voice went on: 'Has the other matter been attended to?'

'Yes,' answered the solicitor. 'Rabson arranged it during the night. I saw him directly I got your message.'

'Good!' came the reply. 'Then I think we're fairly safe.'

'There was a man from the Yard here this morning,' said Mr. Hake, 'asking a lot of questions. I'm rather scared.'

'Nonsense!' said his listener impatiently. 'There's nothing to be scared about, not if we play our cards properly.'

'I think I'd better see you, all the same,' said the lawyer. 'I can't say all I want to say over the telephone.'

'I'll be at Rabson's at three this afternoon,' answered the other, and there was a click as the receiver was hung up.

Mr. Hake pushed aside the instrument, took out his handkerchief with a trembling hand and wiped his damp face. He knew that Mrs. Berman's hours were numbered, and he had not yet got over the shock occasioned by the deaths of Sir James Maddox and William Sneath!

12

At the Bently Buildings

The Bently Buildings were at one time nothing more nor less than a collection of tenement houses in such a bad state of repair that they had been condemned by the local council. An enterprising gentleman had, however, bought the property, and with the expenditure of very little money, for he used most of the old material over again, converted the dilapidated and ramshackle houses into an unpleasant drab-coloured building, which he glorified by having his own name painted across the front in large black letters.

The flats — there were twenty-four of them in all — stood in a mean little street that led off the High Road, Kilburn. They were very respectable, if rather smoke-grimed, and they boasted in the dark and dingy vestibule an aged porter whose skin appeared to have absorbed the general tone of the building, for his face was also drab-coloured, except for the relief offered by an artistic touch of purple, which formed his rather large and mis-shapen nose. This was not altogether the result of nature, but had been acquired by long and careful experiment with various brands of beer obtained from the small public-house which stood in the corner of the street, within a few hundred yards of Mr. Bently's edifice.

The tenants of these flats were extremely respectable. Their respectability was vouched for by the aspidistras and lace curtains that graced the windows, for nothing but respectability can live in an atmosphere of aspidistras and lace curtains. It is the outward and visible sign of an inward and spiritual grace.

Peter Escott, pausing on the opposite side of the pavement on that grey and cheerless afternoon, glanced up at the monotonous windows of Bently Buildings, and came to the conclusion that Mr. John Lane's residence was anything but attractive. For a long time he stood there taking stock of the building, and then crossing the road entered the narrow vestibule. Light apparently was rather a precious commodity here, for the dark entrance was obscured by shadows, and no attempt had been made to light the single unshaded bulb that hung in the centre of the white-washed ceiling.

The reporter looked about him, and presently made out a stone staircase guarded by a green-painted iron hand-rail that zigzagged upwards into the gloom above. At the foot of this against the stone wall was an oak board, on which in faded white letters, were painted the names of the various tenants, together with the numbers of the flat they occupied. Peter went over and with some difficulty, for this was the darkest spot in the vestibule, began to read down the list in search of Mr. John Lane. While he was so engaged he heard a shuffling footstep behind him, and turning saw an elderly man regarding him questioningly through a pair of red-rimmed and rather watery eyes. This individual was wearing a very stained and dirty uniform, which Peter concluded at one time had been green.

' 'oo are ye lookin' for?' he asked in a wheezy voice.

This was evidently the porter, and he appeared to fit in very well with the rest of the building.

'I'm looking for Mr. John Lane,' replied the reporter, and at his words the expression on the other's face underwent an extraordinary change.

He frowned and glared at Peter suspiciously. 'Ho, you want to find Mr. John Lane, do ye?' he demanded gruffly. 'Are ye a friend of his?'

'Not exactly a friend,' said the reporter pleasantly. 'But I should rather like to see him.'

'So would a good many people!' growled the janitor. 'I would, for one.'

Peter concluded that Mr. John Lane was not a very popular tenant. 'He lives in Flat 7, doesn't he?' he began, but the porter interrupted him with a peculiar sound that was between a snort and a cough.

' 'e *lived* in Flat 7,' he grunted with a heavy emphasis on the 'lived', 'but 'e ain't

155

livin' there now.'

Peter looked at him quickly. 'Do you mean he's gone?' he asked.

'That's 'zactly what I do mean,' said the porter. 'Cleared hoff, that's what he's done, and let me in for a month's rent in spite of all 'is fine talk!'

Peter was interested. 'When did he go?' he asked.

'Sometime during the night,' answered the man. 'Must 'ave bin, 'cos I saw 'im come in about eleven, and when I went up this mornin', he was gone, and a lot of 'is things with 'im. Done me for five pounds, 'e 'as.'

Peter thought rapidly. This sudden flight looked very suspicious.

'Does 'e owe you money, too?' asked the porter sympathetically.

'No, I want to see him on quite another matter,' answered the reporter. 'Have you got a key to his flat?'

'I've got a key to h'all the flats,' replied the man. 'Why?'

'I should like to look at his flat, if it could be managed,' said Peter, but at this the porter looked doubtful.

'I don't know as you can do that,' he muttered. 'Supposin' he was to come back arter all? If he found I'd been lettin' strangers into 'is flat, I'd get in trouble.'

Peter decided on a little bluff. 'Look here,' he said confidentially. 'I'm a detective and I'm rather interested in Mr. Lane's movements.' He casually produced a ten-shilling note, and twisted it about in his fingers. 'It is very necessary that I should have a look round his flat.'

The porter eyed the note longingly. 'Wot's 'e bin doin' now?' he enquired.

'He may not have been doing anything,' answered Peter. 'You must clearly understand that I've nothing at the moment against Mr. Lane. I should like to have seen him, but since that is impossible it would help me very greatly if I could have a look round his flat.'

The porter scratched his head, but his cupidity apparently got the better of his scruples. 'Orl right,' he said. 'I'll let yer in. Wait a minute while I gets me keys.'

He shuffled away through a door under the staircase, and after a long delay

157

reappeared with a bunch of keys in his hands.

''is flat's on the third landing,' he said, leading the way up the narrow and worn stairs. Eventually he paused before a narrow green-painted door on the left of a landing and unlocking it pushed it open.

'There you are,' he said. 'Mind 'ow you go. There's a step down you can't see it in the dark.'

'Wouldn't it be possible to have some light?' suggested Peter.

Apparently this had not struck the man before, but he admitted that it was possible, and proved it by pressing down a switch just inside the front door. The narrow hall of Lane's flat became illuminated. It was a bare-looking place: the plain distempered walls were unrelieved by pictures of any kind, and the cracked plaster showed patches of dirt. A row of hooks had been nailed against one wall, for the reception of coats and hats, but these were empty. The floor was covered with a strip of ragged linoleum, and just inside the door were the remains of a mat. Facing the front door was another door, and two others flanked it on either side.

'That's the kitchen,' volunteered the porter, pointing to the door directly facing them. 'The right 'and one's the sitting-room and t'other's the bedroom.'

'I'll look at the sitting-room first,' said Peter, opening the door.

The room into which he was looking was small and oblong in shape. To his right was a fireplace with the remains of a burnt-out fire, and on his left a large square window that obviously overlooked the street. A dingy carpet covered the floor, a large portion of bare boards being visible all round it. Of furniture there was very little. A broken-down basket chair, a table covered with a strip of green cloth on which the remains of a meal had been laid on some sheets of newspaper, and a cheap sideboard of plain oak constituted the bulk. On this stood half-a-dozen empty beer bottles, and a plate containing some apples. Evidently John Lane's poverty had not been exaggerated, thought Peter as he gazed at the room.

A close inspection revealed that the mantelpiece was littered with a varied collection of objects: pipes, a half-used tin of tobacco, a packet of cheap cigarettes in which two remained, an empty match box, a broken lighter, and the most interesting of all, a heap of summonses. He ran through the latter quickly. Some were old and some were recent; two were from the Gas Company and several from various tradespeople. One was a High Court Judgment Summons for the sum of three hundred and sixty pounds taken out by a firm calling themselves McIntyre and Co. Peter smiled as he saw this, for he knew the firm. They were moneylenders with offices in Sackville Street, run by a gentleman who had been born with the name of Goldstein.

He made a rough calculation of the amounts, and discovered that John Lane's total indebtedness, so far as the summonses went anyway, amounted to close on seven hundred pounds. Quite an unpleasant sum to have hanging round one's neck, particularly as it seemed that Mr. Lane would have found it difficult to lay his hands on seven hundred pence. There was ample evidence here of a motive for the murder of his uncle — if he had known that the death of Sir James would enrich him to the extent of five thousand pounds. But had he known? Was he aware of the contents of the will? Peter was not sure of this, but he felt that the flight of John Lane was certainly suspicious. He replaced them where he had found them and turned his attention to the rest of the room, but he found nothing more of interest and under the curious eyes of the porter came out and went into the bedroom.

If anything it was smaller than the sitting-room. A single iron bedstead occupied the space behind the door. Set at an angle in one corner was a wardrobe, and by its side a combination chest of drawers and dressing-table. By the window stood a marble-topped washstand. A worn rug in the centre of the room completed the contents. But what interested Peter mostly was the appalling disorder of the place. All the drawers were open, and shirts, collars, socks and handkerchiefs were strewn about in every direction. A pair of trousers lay crumpled up beneath the window. In the middle of the room was a waistcoat. Flung half on and half off a chair was the jacket belonging to the suit. Everything pointed to a sudden and hasty departure. The bed had not been slept in and on the coverlet could be seen the marks where some square object had rested. Peter turned to the porter who was standing in the doorway, watching him interestedly.

'Do you know if there's anything missing from this room?' he asked.

The man looked about him. 'There used to be an h'old suitcase over there,' he answered pointing to the space under the window. 'It's gone now I noticed that when I came up 'ere this mornin'.'

'I thought there would be something of the kind,' said the reporter. 'These marks on the bed here are evidently where he rested it while he was packing.'

He made a search of the room, but found nothing until he was on the point of leaving. And then he caught sight of a small object that had rolled under the wardrobe. Going back, he stooped and picked it up. It was a small bottle of dark blue glass. There was no cork and the chemist's label had been roughly scratched off. Peter sniffed at the narrow neck. A faint, almost imperceptible smell like rotten apples came to his nostrils, and his forehead wrinkled in a frown. The bottle had contained chloroform. It was an unexpected discovery and it made him think. What had John Lane been doing with a bottle of chloroform? An idea occurred to him that seemed wildly improbable, and yet it accounted for the presence of this bottle. Perhaps Lane had not gone of his own free will after all? Perhaps he, too, like Sir James Maddox and William Sneath, had fallen a victim to some unknown person who lurked in the background behind this extraordinary case?

13

What the Night Watchman Saw

Peter had handled the bottle carefully by its neck, and now he wrapped it in his handkerchief and put it away in his pocket. If there was any truth in the startling idea that occurred to him, there might be finger-prints on the bottle which would prove helpful. He determined to take it to his friend, Mr. Trimmer, and have it tested.

'I've seen all I want to see here,' he remarked, turning to the porter, 'but before I go I'd like to ask you a question or two. First of all, how long has Mr. Lane been living here?'

'A matter of eight months now,' replied the man. 'Gettin' on for nine.'

'Did he have many visitors?' went on the reporter. 'Regular visitors I mean?'

The man smiled sourly. 'Oh yes, 'e 'ad plenty of visitors,' he said. 'Some of 'em was pretty reg'lar too! But I 'ad orders to say 'e was out to all of 'em. Darned nuisance it were too, keepin' on 'avin' to leave me work!'

'He had no friends then who came to see him?' questioned Peter.

The porter shook his head. 'Not that I've ever seen,' he declared. 'The only people wot ever came 'ere for him, was people 'e owed money to. There was plenty of them I can tell you!'

'You said he owed you five pounds. How was that?' said Peter.

'Rent,' said the other laconically. 'Ye see it's like this 'ere. I'm supposed to collect the rents from the people of this 'ere building every week, and at the end of every month Mr. Bently comes round, checks me books, and I 'ands 'im over the cash.'

'I see,' said the reporter. 'How much was Mr. Lane's rent?'

'The same as all the others,' answered the man. 'Twenty-five shillin's a week.'

'So he hadn't paid you for four weeks?'

'No 'e 'adn't,' said the porter gloomily. 'An' it don't look now as though I shall get it, neither. Which means that I'll 'ave to make it good meself.'

'It seems to me,' said Peter, 'that you were rather foolish, knowing Mr. Lane's circumstances, to let him run on without paying.'

'S'pose I was,' agreed the porter. 'But 'e promised faithful 'e'd let me 'ave the full amount before Mr. Bently came round. Said 'is uncle were a rich man, and 'e was goin' to get it from 'im.'

'Oh he said that, did he?' Peter's eyes narrowed. 'Did he mentioned his uncle's name?'

'No,' said the man. 'But 'e pitched a yarn about 'im being a 'Sir', and livin' in a big 'ouse in the country. 'e said they'd 'ad a quarrel. I was a fool to believe 'im, but 'e 'ad a sort of takin' way with 'im.'

Peter rubbed his chin thoughtfully. If John Lane had decided to murder his uncle this story would fit in very well. He couldn't tell the porter that he was expecting to inherit some money, but in order to put him off and so gain time until his scheme had materialised and he was in possession of the five thousand pounds, he had concocted a very plausible story. Once more Peter addressed himself to the porter.

'Do you sleep on the premises?' he asked.

'Yes, in the basement,' answered the man.

'And what time do you go off duty?'

'All depends,' said the porter. 'Sometimes I'm done at 'alf-past ten, sometimes not until nigh on twelve.'

'What time did you finish last night?' asked Peter.

'Just after eleven,' replied the other.

'Did you hear anything during the night?' the reporter continued. 'Any sounds of people moving about?'

'No,' said the man. 'I didn't 'ear nothin.' If I 'ad 'e wouldn't 'ave slipped off so easy!'

'What time do you shut the main door of the buildings?' asked Peter.

'Ten o'clock,' was the reply.

'And if anybody calls after that time to see any of the tenants, what happens?'

'There's a board outside,' explained the

porter, 'with a bell for each flat and the number of it. If anyone comes arter I've shut the main door, they 'as to ring the bell for the flat they wants, an' the people lets them in theirselves.'

So, thought Peter, it would have been quite easy for somebody to have called on Lane after the porter had retired for the night, rung the bell of number seven, and been admitted by Lane himself. Particularly easy if this person was not a stranger but somebody with whom Lane was familiar, and if Lane were not the murderer the method by which the crime had been carried out had already proved that the person responsible was someone that Sir James knew intimately, and therefore might equally be well known to Lane.

There was nothing to be learned from the porter, and later giving the man his ten shillings, Peter left the buildings. He was on the point of turning towards the main road, when in the dusk of the falling evening, he saw a few yards beyond the entrance to the flats, the red lights which marked a spot where the road had been taken up for repair. A little way beyond this was the glow of a coke fire, and an idea suddenly occurring to him, he changed his mind and went in this direction. As he expected the fire came from a bucket standing in front of a watchman's hut, and when he drew nearer he saw the watchman himself trimming the wicks of some more red lanterns to hang on the scaffolding barrier that surrounded the place where the road was up. Peter approached the man and began a casual conversation. By degrees he turned the talk into the channel which interested him.

'How long has this road been up?' he asked.

'Matter of four days now,' said the watchman. 'Didn't think it'd take so long, but we've got to put in a section of new pipe. It's the main gas pipe too. Cracked it were, and leakin' badly.'

'Sounds pretty dangerous,' commented the reporter. 'Have you been on duty all the time?'

The watchman nodded.

'Pretty monotonous job, isn't it?' said

Peter. 'Not much to amuse you at night?'

'All depends where ye'are,' said the watchman. 'It ain't so bad in a main road, there's always plenty goin' on there, but round these 'ere side streets it's pretty quiet.'

'Wonder you don't fall alseep,' said Peter. 'By the way,' he added quickly, as if it had only just struck him, 'you must have been here last night?'

'Course I were,' said the watchman.

'Well, then, perhaps you can help me,' said the reporter. 'I've got a friend of mine living in these flats over there,' he pointed towards Bently Buildings, 'and I thought I saw him at Piccadilly Circus last night. He swears that he didn't go out at all, but I'm certain I didn't make a mistake. Perhaps you can settle the matter. Did anybody come in or go out of the flats before or after twelve?'

'I couldn't say whether anybody did afore,' said the watchman, 'but somebody did arter.' He chuckled hoarsely, and Peter waited for him to go on. 'About 'alf-past two it were, and he was so drunk 'e couldn't scarcely stand. Beautiful 'e were! It was all 'is pals could do to get 'im in the motor.'

Peter's pulses quickened. 'There was a car, was there?' he said. 'That's interesting. My friend's got a car. A two-seater Morris.'

'Well this weren't no two-seater Morris,' said the watchman. 'It was a big car. One of them baloons.'

'A saloon,' corrected Peter. 'That's funny! You wouldn't expect people living in a place like that to have friends with a big car.'

'Just what I thought,' agreed the old man. 'Particularly a car like that one. She wasn't 'alf a beauty. All shinin' silver an' polished paint.'

'And you say the man was drunk?' prompted the reporter.

'Drunk?' echoed the watchman. 'I ain't never seen anyone so drunk! 'e couldn't stand, 'e couldn't. One of 'is pals 'ad to 'old 'im up while the other shut the door of them flats. An' as for walkin', that was beyond 'im. They 'ad to carry 'im to the motor like a sack of 'taters.'

Peter felt that he was getting on. Of

course there was no proof that the drunken man had been John Lane, but coupled with the empty chloroform bottle, the possibility became more than probable. If so, his wild idea was not so wild after all. Somebody had wanted to get John Lane out of the way, and had adopted this means of doing it.

'I suppose you didn't notice the make of the car?' he asked casually.

'Yes I did,' said the watchman. 'It were a Daimler. I know because I went in for that there competition that was runnin' in the papers a few weeks ago. Didn't win nothin' I didn't, but I learnt some'at about cars.'

'A black saloon Daimler,' murmured Peter. 'Must have been a nice car.'

'It were,' said the watchman. 'But I never said it was black, mister. Green it was, one of them light greens. You know, bilious lookin'.'

'I know what you mean,' said Peter, elated at the success of his ruse. 'Well I don't think it could have had anything to do with my friend. I'm sure he doesn't know anybody owning a car like that, besides which he doesn't drink.'

He chatted for a few moments longer, and then wishing the watchman good night, set off for Fleet Street. But he did not go there directly. He went first to Scotland Yard, and spent nearly an hour in Chief-Inspector Trimmer's bare office, talking to that melancholy individual. And when he finally left he had the satisfaction of knowing that before very many hours had passed, every police station in the country and every constable on duty would be looking for a large saloon Daimler car painted a yellowish-green.

14

After the Inquest

The inquest on Sir James Maddox was
held on the following morning, and Peter
attended with Inspector Burnett. The
proceedings were very brief. The medical
evidence regarding the cause of death was
taken, and then the police asked for and
obtained a fortnight's adjournment. Peter
smiled when he heard this, for it showed
that Burnett was still doubtful of Dick
Mason's guilt. Had he not been he would
never have asked for the adjournment to
obtain fresh evidence. The reporter was
allowed to see Dick for a few minutes
after the inquiry was over, and although
he found him a little gloomy at the
prospect of having to remain under
detention, before Peter left he had
succeeded in cheering him up.

'I don't suppose you'll be here very
long,' he said. 'I hope soon to be able to

get you out altogether.'

'It's jolly good of you, Escott, to take all this trouble,' said Dick gratefully. 'It's cheering to know that somebody believes in me, and is doing something.'

'I'm not the only one who believes in you,' said Peter, and the other reddened. 'Keep your spirits up and hope for the best.'

He shook hands and after a few words with Burnett went back to London.

When he had visited Scotland Yard after his interview with the night watchman on the previous day, he had asked Mr. Trimmer among other things, to find out whether anyone by the name of Hardy had been executed during the last twenty years, and earlier that morning before he had left for High Wycombe had received a reply in the negative. No one of that name had been executed, or even remotely connected with any murder. Mrs. Berman, therefore, had lied to the girl when she made that statement. Why?

Peter was unable to find a satisfactory answer to this question except the obvious one that she had said the first thing that had come into her head out of spite, because the girl had tried to prevent her getting in to see Hake. But it was hardly the sort of thing that would be likely to enter the woman's head, unless there was some basis of truth in it. He determined if possible to find Mrs. Berman, and see if he could discover something from her that would throw a light on the mystery. There was no doubt that she and Hake knew something. When the lawyer had whispered to her after she had forced her way into the office, Peter had guessed from the glance she had shot in his direction that Hake had told her who he was, or rather who he was pretending to be, and warned her. That would account for her having become so suddenly subdued.

There was a secret shared between them, and the reporter was pretty certain that it was connected with the death of Sir James. But the finding of Mrs. Berman was not so easy. He 'phoned up Betty, but she could not tell him, and he did not want to ask Hake. It would only arouse the man's suspicions and give him the opportunity of warning the woman before he, Peter, could reach her. He decided to get Mr. Trimmer to help him, and after a hasty visit to the *Megaphone* offices where he turned in a brief account of the inquest, made his way to the Yard, and explained to that lean and gloomy man what he wanted.

'It shouldn't be difficult,' said Mr. Trimmer, puffing at one of his eternal woodbines. 'I'll do my best for you, Peter. What's the idea anyway?'

Peter told him as much as he knew, omitting, however, to mention the subterfuge by which he had gained his interview with the lawyer. The melancholy inspector was interested, and put several questions. Just before leaving Peter asked if there had been any news of the green Daimler, but was told that nothing had come through yet.

He spent the rest of the day at the *Megaphone* offices trying to evolve some theory which would include all the various disconnected scraps of information that he had succeeded in picking up.

It was a little after ten o'clock and he

had just got back to his flat when the telephone bell rang, and picking up the receiver he heard Mr. Trimmer's slow voice come over the wire.

'I've found out that woman's address for you,' said the chief inspector. 'Mrs. Annie Berman her name is, and she lives in a cottage on the Horsham Road. It's called Briar Cottage.'

'Thanks very much,' said Peter. 'You've been quick.'

'We don't let the grass grow under our feet at the Yard,' growled the inspector. 'We can be quick enough when we want to be.'

He rang off, and Peter hung up the receiver and noted down the address on a pad. His first inclination was to go to Horsham then and there, but on second thoughts he realised that by the time he got there the woman would in all probability be in bed. He decided eventually to wait till the morning. He could leave early and get to Horsham soon after nine. Having come to this decision, and feeling very tired, he went to bed. Could he have seen into the

future he would have acted very differ-
ently.

★   ★   ★

Briar Cottage was an unprepossessing
place, but it matched Mrs. Berman's
rather dour personality. It was built of
cold grey stone unrelieved by ivy or
creeper, and set in a wilderness of the
straggling bushes from which it apparently got its name. The interior was as
grim and stark as the exterior, for the
furniture was old and meagre and dated
from that comfortless period known as
early Victorian.

The sitting-room smelt musty and
unused. It was a cheerless place with its
lace antimacassars, and waxen fruit in
great dome-like glass covers, its dejected-
looking aspidistra in a polished brass
bowl, and its shiny horse-hair-covered
chairs and sofa. Mrs. Berman never set
foot inside this room, except to dust it,
and on those rare occasions when she
received visitors, and since these were few
and far between, it was kept mostly shut.

She preferred the kitchen, and certainly this was more comfortable. It was her habit to take a walk every night, wet or fine, along the Horsham Road. She would go slowly, always at the same pace, as far as the crossroads, turn and come back again; in all, a distance of about two miles.

On this particular night, the same on which Chief-Inspector Trimmer had given Peter her address, and a night that was chill and inclined to be windy, with low clouds scudding across the dark sky, she returned from her usual constitutional and let herself into the gloomy cottage. It boasted neither gas nor electricity. The illumination was supplied by one large oil lamp which she carried about with her wherever she went. She opened the front door, and felt her way along the familiar passage to the kitchen, picked up the box of matches which she had left in readiness on the table, and lit the lamp. Poking the dying fire into a blaze, she took off her hat and coat, hung them on the peg behind the door, put the kettle on to boil, and fetching a bottle of gin from a cupboard, produced sugar, a lemon and a glass. With these necessaries for her usual nightcap near at hand, she sat down in her worn old rocking chair, and applied herself to some knitting which she took from a basket on the table at her elbow.

She smiled complacently as the long ivory needles clicked rhythmically, and the smile was induced by the recollection of a conversation she had had with Mr. Hake, a conversation that should result in considerably augmenting the meagre pension that she was at present receiving. After all, she deserved to get something substantial out of the plot. In a way she had been the one to suggest it. It was true that it had been elaborated, but the skeleton of the idea was her own. If they thought they were going to freeze her out they were mistaken. No one had yet succeeded in getting the better of Annie Berman. The sum she had asked, though a large one, was small compared with what they would make, and it had been her idea — entirely her idea — at the beginning.

As her large, bony fingers plied the

needles skillfully, her mind was busy with what she would do with the money that would soon be hers. The kettle boiling over and hissing into the fire brought her attention back to the present. She rose, mixed her hot gin, and returning to her chair, put aside her work, and sipped the steaming fluid with enjoyment. She had two glasses of the hot concoction, and as she set the empty tumbler down and was considering whether she would have a third, she heard the hum of a car as it passed by the cottage along the mainroad. There was nothing unusual in this, and she scarcely paid any attention to it. The sound of the engine dwindled in the distance, and the silence of the night gathered close once more. She had her third glass, and then with a glance towards the clock, rose to go to bed.

And then her throat contracted, and her small eyes widened in fear, for the kitchen door which had been closed, was slowly opening! The scream that welled up from the depths of her terror-laden soul was choked and strangled by the dryness of her throat. Motionless, she stared with a horrid fascination at that slowly moving door. It opened wider, wider yet, and a dim and shadowy figure loomed in the gloom of the passage beyond. A ray of light from the table lamp, shining through a torn hole in the opaque shade, fell upon the face under the brim of the slouch hat, and the woman found her voice.

'You!' she croaked faintly. 'You! What are you doing here?'

'You know very well what I'm doing here,' hissed a low voice, the voice that had spoken to Hake over the telephone. 'I'm here because of your threats. I allow nobody to threaten me twice!'

She crouched back as the man advanced into the room. 'I didn't mean nothin',' she whimpered. 'I didn't, honestly. I wouldn't squeal, you know that!'

'You won't get the chance!' he snarled, and the thin scream that came from her lips died to a husky moan as his strong hands found and gripped her skinny throat.

She fought feebly, beating at his face with her clenched fists, but a flame-shot curtain of blackness was closing down on her relentlessly.

. . . A roaring noise, like gallons of water rushing over a weir, sounded in her ears, and then — nothing . . .

The murderer dropped her limp body to the floor, and wiped his streaming face. For a moment he stood looking down at the huddled, motionless thing, and then, leaving the kitchen, he made his way out of the cottage as silently as he had entered it, and was lost in the darkness of the night.

Faintly on the stillness came the whine of a motor engine, which presently blended with the wind and faded away into silence.

15

The Press Cuttings

'There's no doubt as to the cause of death,' remarked the police doctor, rising to his feet. 'She was strangled.'

Peter Escott did not require his verdict to tell him that. One glance at the woman's face as she lay sprawling on the kitchen floor was sufficient.

'How long has she been dead?' asked the grey-haired man who was with him, and the doctor shrugged his shoulders.

'It's difficult to say within an hour or so,' he replied. 'But at least six hours and not more than twelve.'

The local superintendent of the Horsham division scratched his chin. 'It's a nasty business,' he said, shaking his head. 'You've no idea, I suppose, Mr. Escott, who was responsible for the crime?'

'No,' answered the reporter. 'As I told you, I came down in the hope of being able to get something out of her concerning the Maddox murder. I wish now I'd come last night.'

It was a little after ten o'clock in the morning, and Peter, the hastily-summoned doctor, and the local police superintendent were standing in the dead woman's kitchen. Peter had left London early for Horsham, but all attempts at getting an answer to his knocking and ringing at the cottage had been without result. He had thought at first that Mrs. Berman had left, or gone out early, but exploring in the rear of the place, had happened to glance in through the window of the kitchen, and had seen the ugly, silent figure crumpled up by the fireplace. He had immediately informed the police, and an entrance had been effected by the sitting-room window, which was partly open.

'I've read about that case.' The superintendent twisted his face into an expression of thought. 'That was a queer business, too. What connection had she with it?' He jerked his head towards the body.

'She was in the employment of the

dead man at one time,' answered Peter. 'She was his daughter's nurse. When the girl grew up and a nurse was no longer required, she was pensioned off.'

'And you expected to get something out of her?' The superintendent raised his eyebrows. 'What did you think she could tell you?'

'I don't know what she could have told me,' replied the reporter, 'but I was under the impression that she knew something.'

'I didn't know there was any mystery in the matter,' put in the doctor. 'I thought the police had got the man who killed Maddox. Wasn't he found by that secretary fellow just after he had murdered the old man?'

'Yes, but I don't think they're quite certain,' said Peter, a little evasively.

'If the death of this woman has got anything to do with the other affair,' said the superintendent, 'it looks as if they were right. That chap they've detained can't have killed her, because he's locked up.' He rubbed the side of his nose with his knuckle. 'Do you know if she had any relations or friends we could get in touch with?'

'I know nothing about her beyond what I've told you,' declared Peter. 'Most likely Mr. Hake, of Hake, Rand & Hake could help you. He was Sir James Maddox's solicitor, and also acted for Mrs. Berman.'

The superintendent made a note in his book, and as he closed it with a snap a constable came in to say that the ambulance had arrived. It carried away both the body of Mrs. Berman, and the doctor, and when it had gone the superintendent began a search of the cottage. Peter had asked and obtained permission to remain, and he followed the examination with interest. The state of the place was a testimony to the dead woman's passion for neatness — everything was in its proper place, and there wasn't a speck of dust anywhere. In spite of the fact that she had been a heavy drinker — they found twenty empty bottles of gin and three full ones ranged neatly along the walls of the pantry — she had not let this interfere with her housework.

Nothing of interest was found until the

superintendent came to an old-fashioned walnut bureau in the sitting-room. It contained mostly a collection of paid and unpaid household bills, and some cheap stationery and envelopes. But in a lower drawer the police official found a roll of press cuttings. They were dusty and yellow with age, and the date of the paper from which they had been taken was twenty-one years previously. Peter looked at the headlines and saw with a start of surprise that the cuttings were an account of the trial of a man named Henry Skiller for the murder of an elderly grocer in his shop in a London suburb. Together with the superintendent, he skimmed through the thick wad, and came upon a smaller cutting that stated briefly that Henry Skiller had been duly executed. Peter frowned. Why had the dead woman kept these things so carefully? His mind flew back to Hake's office and the scene with Betty. 'The daughter of a man wot was 'ung!' He could hear the shouted taunt again clearly. Had it been of Henry Skiller the woman was talking, and was Betty Hardy his daughter? There was nothing impossible in the suggestion, but what had it to do with Mrs. Berman? What interest had she in the girl? The further Peter got with this case, the more involved it became. Each fresh development only served to make the thing more mysterious. The death of Sir James, the murder of William Sneath in the taxicab, the disappearance of John Lane, and now the killing of this woman. How did they all fit in, and what was behind it?

The voice of the superintendent broke in on the reporter's thoughts. 'Queer she should have kept those things,' he said. 'I remember that case well. I hadn't long joined the force, and I used to read up all the crime cases, thinking they'd be useful to me later on, and I remember the Skiller murder. There was a petition got up to try and save him being hanged on the grounds that he was mad and not responsible, but it fell through. I wonder why she kept those cuttings?'

'I should like to know that, too,' replied Peter.

'Well, they can't have anything to do

with this business,' the superintendent went on, continuing his search, 'but it's funny, all the same.'

He took something out of the drawer in which he had found the cuttings, and stared at it.

'This is more likely to help,' he said. He held out a cheap and faded photograph. It was the picture of a youngish-looking man, with dark, well-oiled hair brushed into a quiff across his forehead. He was standing by a carved table, one hand resting on a book, the usual pose beloved by the photographer of several years ago. Written across one corner with ink that had faded to a light brown with age, were the words: 'With love from Frank.'

Peter turned the photograph over. On the back in the same handwriting was written: 'Frank Rabson, 9 Edgeley Street, Camden Town.'

'Might be worth while to try and trace this man's present whereabouts,' said the superintendent, when Peter pointed this out. 'Perhaps he can tell us something.'

'He shouldn't be difficult to trace,' said the reporter, and then, as an idea struck him: 'Was Skiller married?'

The superintendent shook his head. 'No,' he said, and his eyes twinkled. 'I think I can see what you're getting at, but he wasn't. You were thinking that perhaps this woman, Berman, might have been his wife?'

That was exactly the idea that had flashed across the reporter's mind, but the superintendent's reply had squashed it.

'Well, I don't think there's anything more to be found here,' said that individual, turning away from the bureau. 'The photograph may help. Of course, the murder may have been done by an ordinary burglar. It's pretty clear that he came in by the sitting-room window, and we can't tell if there was anything stolen or not.'

He continued his search of the cottage, but nothing else in the nature of a clue came to light, and after leaving a constable in charge he took his departure.

Peter drove him as far as the police station, and then making his way to the nearest post office, telephoned a report of the murder to the *Megaphone*. It was just a bare account, and contained nothing concerning the newspaper cuttings, or the dead woman's connection with the Maddox crime. When he had done this, he began to realise that he was hungry, and went into a restaurant for something to eat.

During the meal he considered his next move. He was rather anxious to get an interview with Frank Lane, but there were difficulties in the way. Lane was hardly likely to welcome the appearance of a reporter, and less likely to part with any information even if Peter was able to get in to see him. By the time he had finished his lunch, he had decided on what he would do. Going back to the post office, he put a call through to High Wycombe, and succeeded in getting on to Inspector Burnett. After giving the Inspector a brief account of the tragedy at Briar Cottage, he arranged to meet him at his flat that afternoon. Burnett came half an hour after Peter had got home, and to him the reporter gave a detailed account of everything that had happened up to the present.

'We'll go and see this man Lane together,' said Burnett when he had finished, and since this was exactly what Peter had been hoping for, he agreed with alacrity.

They arrived at the rather elegant block of flats in which Mr. Frank Lane lived just after five, and entering the vestibule, were carried up to the fifth floor in the lift. A manservant opened the polished rosewood door in answer to Burnett's ring, and respectfully enquired what they wanted.

'Will you take my card to Mr. Lane,' said the inspector, 'and ask him if I can have a few words with him?'

The man, who seemed a combination of butler and valet, ushered them into the square, well-furnished hall, and departed on his errand. He returned after a very short delay, and requested them to follow him. Tapping lightly on a door at the end of the hall, he held it open and ushered the inspector and Peter into a small, but well-furnished room, and into the presence of a thin man who rose from a low chair in front of an electric fire at their entrance.

'I can guess why you wish to see me,' said Mr. Frank Lane, twisting the card that Burnett had sent in between his fingers. 'It is, of course, in connection with the death of my uncle. A dreadful affair, dreadful!'

He waved his hand towards two chairs, looking rather hard at Peter as he did so.

'Now,' he said when they were seated. 'What can I do for you?'

'The first thing I should like to know, sir,' said Burnett, 'is your exact movements on the night of the murder. Merely as a matter of routine,' he added hastily, as Mr. Lane looked rather startled. 'I just want to make certain that I have the correct times. I understand that you left Maddox Court at a quarter to eleven.'

'That's quite right.' Mr. Lane inclined his head. 'My chauffeur can bear out the time.'

'I don't think there'll be any necessity for that, sir,' smiled the inspector. 'Now on that night you had dinner with Sir

James. Did you notice anything in his demeanour that was different from the usual?'

'Nothing,' replied Lane.

'He said nothing at all,' Burnett went on, 'that might suggest that he was in the least degree apprehensive, or was expecting the fate that was so soon to overtake him?'

'No, so far as I was concerned,' was the reply. 'He was exactly the same as usual.'

'You say so far as you were concerned,' said the inspector quickly. 'Does that mean that his manner was different to anyone else's?'

'No, no!' Mr. Lane hastened to correct himself. 'I used the words unthinkingly. What I meant was that I had noticed no difference in him personally.'

'I see,' said Burnett. He paused for a moment, and Peter took up the interrogation.

'I believe you have a younger brother, Mr. Lane?' he said. 'Could you tell us something about him?'

The other's face clouded, and for the first time he hesitated.

'What exactly do you wish to know about him?' he asked presently.

'Anything you can tell us,' replied the reporter. 'Wasn't there some sort of a quarrel between him and Sir James?'

'They weren't very good friends,' admitted Mr. Lane reluctantly, and then quickly: 'I hope you haven't any idea of associating John with this business. He's rather weak in some things, but I can assure you absolutely incapable of a crime like that.'

'Have you seen him lately, sir?' asked Burnett.

'I'm afraid I've not,' said the other, shaking his head. 'We — well, we don't agree very well. He has his views on things and I have mine, and they're very different.'

'What is the make of your car?' asked Peter suddenly.

The abrupt change of subject caused Mr. Lane to stare at him in blank astonishment. 'The make of my car?' he repeated. 'It's a Daimler, why?'

'What colour is it?' asked the reporter, without answering his question.

'Green,' said Mr. Lane, looking at him as though he had suddenly taken leave of his senses. 'Really, I cannot understand the reason for these questions.'

'It may help you to understand better,' said Peter, 'when I tell you that your brother has disappeared from his flat in Bently Buildings, and that we have every reason to suppose that he went away in a green Daimler.'

'Good God!' In his agitation, Mr. Lane started to his feet, and began to walk quickly up and down the small room. 'Are you serious?'

'Perfectly serious,' replied the reporter. 'He left the night before last.'

'Then it couldn't have been my car,' declared Mr. Lane quickly. 'I haven't used my car for four days.'

'It would be impossible for anyone to take it out without your knowledge, sir?' asked the inspector.

'Quite impossible,' said the other. 'I keep it in a large garage in an adjoining street, and nobody except myself or my chauffeur could get hold of it.'

'I should like to make certain of that

point, sir,' said Burnett. 'Would you mind ringing through to your garage, and letting me have a word with the manager?'

'I'll do so at once.' Frank Lane went over to a telephone that stood on a desk by the window, and gave a number. After a few seconds' delay he called over his shoulder to the inspector.

'Here you are,' he said, 'the manager of the garage is here now.'

Burnett went over and took the receiver from his hand. After a short conversation he hung up the black cylinder.

'Well, that settles that, sir,' he said. 'It evidently wasn't your car that called so late at Bently Buildings and took Mr. John Lane away.'

'It's a most extraordinary thing altogether,' said Mr. Lane, still walking up and down with a worried expression. 'Most extraordinary! I'm sure John had no friends likely to possess a car, much less an expensive car like the one you've described.'

'The people who took him away may not have been friends,' put in Peter.

Frank Lane stopped, and looked at him

quickly. 'You mean — ' he began, and left the sentence unfinished.

'I mean,' explained the reporter, 'there are two alternatives. One is that John Lane left the Bently Buildings for purposes of his own, and of his own free will; the other is that he was taken away forcibly for some reason or other by some people who may or may not be connected with the murder of Sir James Maddox.'

He mentioned the evidence of the night watchman and the discovery of the chloroform bottle.

'That rather tends to discount the probability of the first suggestion,' he went on, 'and leaves us with the second and the further questions: Who wanted John Lane out of the way? Why? And where have they taken him?'

'This is all amazing to me,' said Mr. Lane, shaking his head. 'I was under the impression that the murder of my uncle was quite a simple affair, and that the police had got the man who did it. But what you tell me seems to throw quite a different light on the matter.'

'It does, sir,' said Burnett. 'We thought

it was a simple affair at first, but this man Mason can't have been responsible for the other two crimes, because at the time they were committed he was under lock and key in the police station at High Wycombe.'

'Other two crimes?' said Lane in surprise.

The inspector nodded. 'Yes, sir. A 'nose' — police informer,' he corrected himself hastily, 'called William Sneath has been murdered, and Miss Maddox's old nurse, Annie Berman.'

'Old Annie murdered!' exclaimed Frank Lane. 'Good God! When did this happen?'

'Last night,' said Peter, and he told him of the discovery. 'There seems little doubt,' he concluded, 'that these three crimes are connected.'

'But why should anyone wish to kill Mrs. Berman?' said Frank Lane. 'Nobody could benefit by her death.'

'I suppose you knew her fairly well, sir?' said Burnett.

'I was constantly seeing her, of course,' answered Lane, 'during the time she was Margaret's nurse, that is. But I know nothing about her private life. Nothing at all. And it's some years now since I saw her.'

'Did you ever hear her mention the name of Henry Skiller?' asked Peter.

Mr. Lane shook his head.

'Or anyone of the name of Hardy?' said the reporter.

'No,' answered the other, frowning. 'I seem to have heard the last name, though, somewhere.'

'Probably in connection with Sir James's solicitors,' said Peter. 'Mr. Hake has a secretary named Betty Hardy.'

Frank Lane's face cleared. 'Yes, that's it,' he replied. 'I knew I'd heard the name.'

They asked him several more questions regarding Mrs. Berman, but without adding in any way to their meagre stock of knowledge concerning the dead woman. And presently they took their leave.

It was a peculiar coincidence that Frank Lane's car should be the same in colour and make as that seen by the night watchman outside the Bently Buildings, on the night of John Lane's disappearance. And yet it could not have been the same unless the manager of the garage was lying, and there was no reason to suppose that he was. However, they decided to make sure, and after leaving Lane's flat, called at the garage and interviewed the manager personally. The result of this proved beyond doubt that Lane's green Daimler had not been out on the night in question, or for several nights previously. They had not only the manager's assertion for this, but the confirmation of two mechanics, and Mr. Lane's own chauffeur, who happened to be at the garage working on a minor repair to the car. Still, it certainly was a curious thing that the car which had called for John Lane should have been a green Daimler. Was it pure accident, or was there a definite purpose behind the choice? If so, the purpose was plain. The people who had chosen that particular colour and make of car must have done so with the object of trying to throw suspicion on Frank Lane, and yet they must have realised that an enquiry at the garage would settle the matter. Or didn't they know? Were they under the impression that Lane's car *would* be out that night?

Peter, who had worked this out in the solitude of his flat after leaving Burnett, decided to settle this point at once, and put through a telephone call to Frank Lane.

'I'm sorry to trouble you again, Mr. Lane,' he said when he heard the other's voice at the end of the wire, and explained who he was. 'But could you tell me whether you had any intention of going anywhere on the evening of November the 16th?'

'As a matter of fact, I had,' was the reply, 'but feeling rather unwell, I put the engagement off.'

'Do you mind telling me where you were going?' said Peter.

'Not at all,' answered the other. 'I was going to dine with Mr. Hake. He wanted to talk over some matters connected with my uncle's death, and asked me to dine with him for that purpose.'

'Where does he live?' asked the reporter.

'At West Hill, Sydenham,' answered Mr. Lane.

'So if you had gone,' continued Peter, 'you would naturally have used your car?'

'Yes,' was the rather surprised reply.

'Thank you, that's all I wanted to know,' said the reporter, and he hung up the receiver.

So Hake had expected that Lane would be out in the green Daimler that night. Had, in fact, gone to some trouble to make sure that this would be the case. Was that invitation to dinner prompted solely with the idea of discussing legal matters, or had the disappearance of John Lane already been decided upon, and the invitation issued with the intention of destroying any alibi that Frank Lane might have concerning the green Daimler?

16

The Green Daimler

'This is the National Programme from London. Before reading the second general news bulletin, I have a police message. Wanted: Any information concerning a green painted Daimler saloon car, number unknown. This car was in the vicinity of Kilburn on the night of November the 16th. Will anyone who saw this car, or who can give any information regarding it, kindly communicate with Chief Detective-Inspector Trimmer, New Scotland Yard, Telephone Number, Victoria 1212, or with any police station . . . Here is the weather forecast for to-night and to-morrow. A deep depression centred over Northern Ireland is moving slowly eastward . . . '

The millions of people who possess wireless sets in the British Isles heard that message on the evening of the interview with Mr. Frank Lane, but only one man took any particular notice of it.

Mr. Harold Shipman, reading his paper after a hard day's work, laid it aside and sat up abruptly as the announcer's voice reached his ears. Mr. Shipman was always interested in SOS and police messages, but this interested him more than usual because it affected him very closely. He knew, or he thought he knew, all about that green Daimler, and during his leisurely supper he turned over in his mind what he had better do about it, with the result that nine o'clock on the following morning found him in the bare and cheerless entrance hall of Scotland Yard, enquiring of the uniformed attendant the way to Chief Detective-Inspector Trimmer's office. He was asked to state his business, and having stated it, was conducted into a large and equally bare waiting-room, from the green-washed walls of which portraits of long-deceased officials stared down at him with accusing eyes. At the expiration of two minutes he was rescued from this depressing atmosphere by another uniformed messenger, who shepherded him along a labyrinth of cold stone corridors, and up innumerable flights of stairs until he was eventually ushered into a room very much the same in appearance as the waiting-room, except that it was smaller, and contained no glowering portraits on the walls. He was left to stare at a thin man sitting behind a large, flat-topped desk. This gloomy individual looked at the nervous Mr. Shipman, and waved him into a chair that stood in front of the desk.

'Sit down, sir,' he said in a lugubrious voice.

Mr. Shipman sat down.

'Now, sir,' said Inspector Trimmer, drawing a paper and pencil towards him, 'I believe you have some information to give us regarding a green Daimler car?'

'That's right,' said Mr. Shipman.

'Give me your full name and address, please,' said the inspector mournfully.

Mr. Shipman gave it, feeling as though he had been charged with murder at least, and not quite certain when he would be told that 'anything he said would be taken down and used in evidence against him.'

'Now then,' said Mr. Trimmer, waiting patiently and getting nothing more at all from the man in front of him. 'What have you to tell me?'

Mr. Shipman cleared his throat, scratched the side of his nose and frowned. 'I think I know this car that you were asking about on the wireless last night,' he volunteered at length.

'You do, eh?' said the inspector sadly. 'Well, what do you know about it?'

'I think it's mine,' said Mr. Shipman.

The lean man in front of him raised his eyebrows wearily. 'Yours?' he said. 'Dear me, that's very interestin', very interestin'. Were you in Kilburn on the night of November the 16th?'

The other shook his head. 'No. You see, it's like this,' he explained. 'I've got a car hiring business in the Edgware Road, and the car you were enquiring about is one of half a dozen that I let out on hire.'

'I see.' Mr. Trimmer nodded slowly, and made a note on the paper in front of him. 'Is this your own business, Mr. Shipman?'

'Yes,' was the reply.

'An' you think,' continued the inspector, 'that this car which we're searchin' for was one of yours?' Mr. Shipman nodded. 'Yes,' he replied. 'I'll tell you why. About half past eight on the night you were enquiring about — '

'November the 16th,' put in the inspector, yawning.

'That's right,' agreed Mr. Shipman. 'As I was saying,' he continued, 'about half past eight on the evening of November the 16th, a man came to my garage and said he wanted to hire a car.'

'What was he like?' asked the inspector.

Mr. Shipman looked at him a little doubtfully. 'I don't know that I could describe him very well,' he said. 'He was thinnish, of medium height, and had a sort of ginger-coloured moustache.'

'The colour of his eyes?' asked Mr. Trimmer, with his own almost completely closed.

'I couldn't tell you,' said the other.

'Know him again if you saw him?' enquired the inspector.

'Yes, I think so,' said Mr. Shipman cautiously. 'He was dressed in a rather soiled macintosh, and wore a soft hat which he kept pulled well down over his eyes.'

'Go on,' said Mr. Trimmer gently as he stopped and hesitated.

'Well,' he continued, 'as I told you, he wanted to hire a car. He said he wanted to take it away with him then and there, and that he would probably want it until the following afternoon. He said he was going to drive a party down to Brighton. I was rather doubtful about letting him have it at first, because he didn't look the sort of man who could afford to go about hiring expensive cars. I said I was afraid he couldn't have it unless he paid a substantial deposit. He made no bones about this, but took a roll of notes from his pocket, and offered to leave me what I wanted. I named a sum, he counted out the money and I gave him a receipt for it. He made a particular point, which I thought was queer at the time, of having the green Daimler. It's the only car of that colour that I've got, and it's not nearly such a good one, or as new, as the others. But he said that he'd taken a fancy to the colour, and that he wanted that one. Well he'd made no trouble about the deposit, so I let him have it, and he drove it away.' He paused, and Mr. Trimmer, who had been taking down his statement in writing, looked up.

'Do you usually allow your cars to be taken out without your own driver?' he asked.

'Oh, yes,' answered the other. 'That's my usual method of business. I advertise that cars can be hired from me with or without a driver. However, to continue, about two o'clock on the following afternoon he brought the car back. I returned him the amount of his deposit less the cost of hire, and that concluded the matter. I thought no more about it, until I heard the message broadcast last night, and thought I'd better come along and say what I knew.'

'You did quite right,' said Mr. Trimmer dolefully. 'Quite right. I suppose you can't add anythin' to this description of the man that I've got here?'

'I'm afraid I can't,' said Mr. Shipman.

'If you can wait for a few minutes,' said

the inspector, 'I'd like to come round to your garage an' see this car.'

'Certainly,' agreed Mr. Shipman willingly. He pulled out his cigarette case and offered one to the inspector, but Mr. Trimmer shook his head. 'Never smoke anythin' but these,' he answered and withdrew from his waistcoat pocket a packet of Woodbines.

Lighting one, he pulled the telephone towards him, and gave the number of Peter's flat. There was no reply, and he tried the *Megaphone* offices. Here he was luckier, for the reporter had just come in. After a short conversation he hung up the receiver, and sat smoking in silence, while Mr. Shipman rather uneasily wondered what was going to happen next. Somebody by the name of Peter Escott had been asked to come along at once, and he concluded that it was this person that they were waiting for.

Peter put in an appearance at the expiration of fifteen minutes, having broken all the traffic regulations in his rush from Fleet Street, and to him Mr. Trimmer briefly repeated the garage owner's narrative.

'We're goin' along to the garage now, Peter,' he concluded, getting up and struggling into his overcoat. 'I sent for you because I thought you'd like to come along with us.'

A long police car took them to Edgware Road, Peter's little machine being left at the Yard. The entrance to Mr. Shipman's business premises was down a narrow cobble-stoned alley, between a greengrocer's and a hire-purchase shop. The words 'Garage, Cars for Hire,' graced the entrance in large red letters, which were apparently illuminated at night with neon lights. The police driver swung the car into this narrow passage, and brought it to a halt at the end, where it widened into a large square, concrete-paved, glass-roofed building which was the garage proper. There were several cars standing in rows, and leading the way past a small kiosk that obviously served as an office, Mr. Shipman pointed to one of these.

'That's the car,' he said.

Mr. Trimmer stood and looked at it for a moment. 'Has this car been out since?' he asked.

The garage proprietor shook his head.

'Cleaned?'

'No,' said Mr. Shipman. 'It hasn't been touched. As a matter of fact, it's due for cleaning this afternoon.'

The melancholy inspector passed his fingers lightly along the radiator. There was only the slightest perceptible film of dust.

'Whoever had this car out,' he remarked, 'certainly didn't go very far if it hasn't been cleaned since he brought it back.'

'Well, I can assure you it hasn't,' said Mr. Shipman. 'That's exactly as it was returned to me.'

The inspector nodded, and opening the door, peered into the interior. If there had been any doubt in his mind that this was the car that had taken John Lane from the Bently Buildings, it vanished at that moment. There was no mistaking the faint, almost imperceptible smell which still clung to the corded upholstery. It was chloroform. He mentioned his discovery in a low voice to Peter, and the reporter nodded. Under the interested eye of Mr. Shipman they made a careful examination of the inside of the car, paying particular attention to the driver's seat, but they found nothing except that the mileage indicator, which they learned from the garage proprietor had been set at nought before the car was taken out, now registered twenty. The car then, during the time it had been in the possession of the unknown man, had travelled twenty miles. Where?

Peter was considering this question, when he noticed a patch of some sticky substance on the wheels. With the aid of his penknife he detached a portion of this, and looked at it more closely. It had a consistency like thick treacle, and gave off a strong tar-like odour, but it was different in appearance to any tar the reporter had ever seen.

'Have you any idea what this is?' he asked Mr. Shipman, and rather to his surprise the latter nodded.

'Yes,' he said, 'that's the new road dressing they're experimenting with.

White tar, they call it.'

Peter said nothing, but his eyes glinted. Shortly after, Mr. Trimmer concluded his examination of the car, and they returned to the Yard.

Peter was itching to put the idea that had occurred to him into practice, and as soon as he conveniently could he took leave of his friend and drove to the *Megaphone* offices. Here he put a call through, and presently was speaking to an official at the County Hall. After being referred to various departments, he at length secured the information that he was seeking. The only piece of road that had been treated by the new white tar process, within a radius of ten miles from the garage in Edgware Road, was Wharfe Street, a narrow road running parallel with the river at Battersea. Peter felt a twinge of excitement as he heard the locality. Battersea! William Sneath had lived at Battersea, and this car which had called at Bently Buildings and departed bearing with it John Lane, had also gone to Battersea. In no other way could it have picked up the patches of road dressing which smothered the wheels. That was an enormous piece of luck. Without that white tar it would have been next to impossible to trace the destination of the green Daimler. It was a small item which the people behind this sinister business had overlooked, and Peter felt that it was going to lead him to the whereabouts of John Lane, and a step nearer to the solution of the mystery.

It was, but it was also to lead him within an ace of death, for in the gloomy neighbourhood of Wharfe Street lurked a menace that was destined very nearly to put an end to his career.

17

The House by the River

Peter Escott drove as far as Victoria, and then looked round for a suitable place in which to garage his car, for during his exploration of Wharfe Street, it was likely to prove more of a liability than an asset. He found a garage, arranged the temporary disposal of the car, and continued the rest of the way to Battersea by bus. He had some little difficulty in finding Wharfe Street, and when by dint of patient enquiry he at length discovered its whereabouts, he was not surprised that few people seemed to know of its existence. It was a narrow thoroughfare set amidst a bristling array of tall chimneys, and ugly square factories. The street itself was lined on either side by ramshackle houses very much in need of repair, the front doors of which opened directly onto dirty pavements. A high wall shut off one end, and Peter thought at first that Wharfe Street was a cul-de-sac, but walking along to the wall he saw that a side street turned off to the left.

He had no difficulty in discovering where the green Daimler had picked up the white tar that plastered its tyres. The piece of road with which the Council had been experimenting with the new dressing was near the beginning of the street, and covered a patch extending for some fifty yards. There was no doubt, therefore, that the car containing John Lane had entered Wharfe Street. The difficulty was to find out which of the sixty or so houses had been its ultimate destination.

Peter walked slowly back along the left-hand side of the street, keeping his eyes fixed on the roadway, but he found nothing to help him. Reaching the end, he crossed the road and began to stroll leisurely back on the opposite side. Here, about halfway down, he had an unexpected piece of luck. Near the edge of the side walk was a splash of black. On the pretence of tying his shoe, Peter stooped, and saw that it had been caused, as he thought, by engine oil soaking into the surface of the roadway. He also saw something else. Close in against the kerb in the half-dried mud of the gutter was the clear impression of a tyre — the lozenge-shaped mark that the tyres of the green Daimler would have made. The car had evidently stopped here, and judging by the oil, stopped for some time. He finished fiddling with his shoe laces, and as he rose to his feet, glanced at the house immediately opposite the place at which the car had stopped. It was different from the others in that it formed the end house of the last block on that side of the street. There was nothing beyond it but the blank wall of a large factory or warehouse, that was broken halfway along its length by high wooden gates. It was not only the last house, but it was also to let. In one of the lower windows was a torn and rather dirty auctioneer's bill. Peter took in as much as he could in a quick glance and then moved away. He had no wish to draw the attention of the inhabitants of Wharfe Street to his interest in the empty house. And he was interested, very interested. He was sure that to that empty house had been brought John Lane — that in all probability, alive or dead, he was in there at the present moment.

As he passed the gates of the factory he noticed the name, 'Lanner & Co., Wholesale Grain Merchants,' painted across the blistered woodwork in faded white letters. It was not, then, as he had thought at first, a factory, but a warehouse. Behind the back of it, and also the empty house, ran the river. He could hear the faint cranking of cranes and derricks, and the long-drawn hoot of a tug. Taking an envelope from his pocket, he made a pretence of copying down the name and address of the grain merchants, while he took in a mental picture of his surroundings. When he had finished he put the envelope back in his pocket and walked briskly up Wharfe Street, along the almost equally narrow thoroughfare that led to it, and so out into the main road. Nothing more could be done while the daylight lasted. The investigation he intended to make at the empty house would have to be undertaken when night had fallen and under cover of darkness.

He went back to Victoria, collected his car, and drove to his flat. So far things had not been going too badly. He had succeeded in tracing the green Daimler to its destination, and had also discovered the whereabouts of John Lane. There was not much doubt in his mind regarding the reason for Lane's disappearance. The people who were behind the plot concerned with the murder of Maddox, had already tried to shift the responsibility of the crime onto one innocent man. When that had, to a large extent, failed, they had tried to repeat the same tactics on another, and but for the presence of the night watchman and the slip they had made in leaving the chloroform bottle behind, might very easily have succeeded. John Lane's sudden disappearance immediately after the murder of his uncle, coupled with the fact that he was up to his eyes in debt, and possessed by no means too good a character, would certainly have rendered him an object for suspicion in the eyes of the police. A great deal of time might have been wasted while their attention was occupied in trying to trace the whereabouts of the missing man. And while they were busy with this false trail the real culprits would have had more chance of covering up their own tracks.

That Hake was deeply involved in the plot was pretty certain. But the question that bothered Peter was what the plot was. The solicitor stood to gain nothing by the death of Sir James; the small legacy he had been left was scarcely sufficient to provide a motive for all this elaborate scheming. Supposing Hake to be the person responsible for all those deaths, what did he gain by it? A possible suggestion offered itself in answer to this question. Hake had been handling all Sir James's affairs. Supposing he had converted a large portion of the dead man's property to his own use, and had murdered his client in order to cover up his depredations, that would provide a very strong and understandable motive.

But if that was the explanation, how

did William Sneath and Mrs. Berman come into it? Had they discovered that Hake had been robbing his client, and tried to make him pay up in order to keep their mouths shut? This was certainly possible. Sneath was known to have added to his slender resources by a little occasional blackmail, and from the scene which Peter himself had witnessed in the lawyer's office, it was obvious that Mrs. Berman had had some sort of hold over Hake. If these two had discovered that he had been carrying out a systematic embezzlement of his client's property, it would not have taken much imagination on their part to connect him with the murder. Indeed, from the evidence of the finger-prints on the glass of the french window at Maddox Court, Sneath had apparently been present, near or actually at the time when the crime had been committed. If he and Mrs. Berman were aware of Mr. Hake's guilt, then there was a very good reason why he should have put them out of the way.

Peter was rather pleased with this theory, although it did not account for the carefully preserved press cuttings in the dead woman's desk at Horsham, or the shot that had so narrowly missed his head in the study at Maddox Court. He thought, however, that an enquiry into Hake's movements on the night of the murder could be worthwhile, and suggested this to Mr. Trimmer on the telephone. That gentleman was in full agreement, and informed Peter that two men had already been put on to keep a watchful eye on Mr. Hake's present movements.

It was getting on for nine o'clock when Peter set about preparing for another visit to the house in Wharfe Street. The night had turned cold, with a faint mist in the air, and although not actually raining, the pavements were wet and the atmosphere unpleasant. The mist increased in density as he neared his destination, and Wharfe Street lay almost hidden under an obscuring blanket of thick white vapour. It was pregnant with the smell of the river, and the faint tang of tarred ropes, and Peter felt that if he had had the choosing of the weather himself, he could not have selected a better night than this for his purpose. It screened his actions effectively from the probable curiosity of the inhabitants of Wharfe Street, and this was just as well, for apart from the fact that somebody in the district might be in league with the people who had abducted John Lane, Peter was proposing to do something that was strictly illegal, and would have been frowned on by his friends in the police.

He met nobody as he made his way down the narrow thoroughfare. Here and there behind the dirty and broken panes of the windows of the miserable houses, a light gleamed, and from somewhere came the cracked strains of an aged wireless set grinding out dance music. But beyond this and the low, mournful wailing of a siren from the direction of the river, there was no sign of sound and life.

He reached the entrance to the empty house and stopped. From his pockets he took a little steel instrument, which had been given him by a notorious burglar whom he had once had occasion to interview. This he inserted in the keyhole of the front door. So long as it was not bolted this should offer him an easy method of ingress. He worked quickly, adjusting the little screw at the end of the pick-lock, until it fitted, and then with a sharp turn of his wrist, he gave it a twist and had the satisfaction of hearing the latch click back. Removing the pick-lock he felt the wards with his fingers, and the suspicion that had flashed through his mind when it had turned so easily, became a certainty. The lock had been recently oiled. It remained to be seen whether the door was bolted as well. Grasping the rusty iron handle, Peter pushed gently, and without a sound the door swung open.

Stepping swiftly across the threshold into the pitch blackness of the hall beyond, he shut the door behind him and stood for a minute listening intently. No sound broke the silence and the darkness was so intense that it could almost be felt. He took a torch from his pocket and sent a gleaming sword of light cutting through the gloom. And as it fell on the broken and bare boards of the passage he experienced a little thrill of satisfaction. In the thick dust which covered the floor were the clear marks of feet, a confused jumble leading from the front door, and vanishing in the direction of the narrow staircase. Someone, more than one, had been here before him, and recently. He moved forward, still keeping the light of his torch on the floor, and followed the trail of foot-prints. They led towards the staircase and then branched off, continuing along by the side of the banisters. Peter paused, flashing his light on the staircase itself, but here the grey powdery surface of the dust remained undisturbed. Obviously the intruders had not gone any higher than the ground floor. He continued to follow the tracks, and they took him down three stairs and through a partly open door into what evidently was the kitchen, for a built-in dresser occupied one wall, and the rusty remains of a cooking stove filled the black cavity of the fire-place. The footprints continued across this room, to a closed door at the opposite end.

Peter opened this, and found himself in

a whitewashed scullery. The lap, lap of water came faintly to his ears, and he concluded that the back of the house must be very close to the river. The footprints here became all massed together, and there was a mark in the dust that looked as though some oblong object had been laid on the floor. This, thought Peter, was where they had put down the unconscious body of John Lane, but what had they done with him after? Had they merely paused here a moment before dropping their victim into the river which ran so conveniently close? He remembered the condition of the kitchen stove. Among that mass of rusty iron it would have been easy to find sufficient loose pieces to weight the pockets of the unconscious man, and so insure that the body would not float.

With this idea in his mind he examined the fastenings of the back door. It was locked and bolted, and the bolts were rusted into their sockets. It only required a glance to show him that this door had not been opened for many months, and so far as he could see, there was no other means of getting out. What, then, had they done with John Lane? He looked about him, and for the first time saw that by the side of the copper there was another door, a narrow door which he had overlooked before, because it fitted closely, and was whitewashed the same as the walls. He went over to it and tugged at the handle, but it was locked and refused to move. Once again the little steel instrument made its appearance. It took him slightly longer to adjust it this time but eventually he managed it, and unlocking the door, pulled it open. A flood of damp-smelling, musty air gushed out, and by the light of his torch he saw that beyond the door a flight of broken wooden steps led down into darkness below. The door was evidently an entrance to a cellar.

He was in the act of stepping through the opening, when a vague warning of danger reached him. He had heard nothing. It was purely subconsciously that he experienced that feeling of the presence of something or someone behind him. He half turned, and at the same instant, a heavy blow struck him full in the centre of his back, and sent him staggering forward. The torch went flying from his hand as he made a vain effort to recover his balance, and then his foot slipped on the topmost step of the cellar stairs, and he fell headlong into the darkness below. His head struck violently against some projecting brickwork, and the blackness that surrounded him rushed like a flood into his brain, and carried away his senses.

18

Facing Death

Peter's senses returned slowly. He passed from complete unconsciousness to an intermediate state which was like the awakening from a heavy sleep. He knew that there was something wrong, and yet was unable to define exactly what it was.

There was a dull throbbing and a lot of pain somewhere, but it was a long time before he discovered that this unpleasing sensation was in his own head.

At first it seemed that the pain was external to himself, that it was there but had no connection with him personally; and then gradually as his shocked brain resumed its normal working, memory returned. He had been in the act of exploring the cellar when something had struck him with tremendous force and pitched him head-long down the stairs. He must have hit his head pretty badly and knocked himself out.

He tried to struggle to his feet, but found, rather to his surprise, that he could not move at all. Impenetrable darkness surrounded him, and in his partially dazed state it was some time before he was able to make out the reason for this strange helplessness. He could neither move his legs nor his arms, and it was borne home to him that he had been securely tied with thick rope. By twisting himself round he was able to feel the rough strands with his fingers. He lay still for a moment to allow the dizziness which the movement had caused to pass off. Who had tied him up like this?

Obviously he had not been alone in the house after all. Although he had seen nothing and heard no sound, somebody had been lurking in the shadows of the empty building watching his every movement. And as he realised this he became annoyed with himself for not having taken more precautions. The house had seemed so utterly deserted that he had taken it for granted that the people who used it were absent, but he realised now that he had been careless. He ought to have made absolutely sure that he had the place to himself before starting on his investigations. He should have searched the place thoroughly and adopted the simple method of bolting the front door on the inside, which would have effectually prevented anybody being able to enter and take him by surprise.

He had been so engrossed in following that trail of foot-prints in the dust that he had overlooked the possibility that there might be others as interested as he was in the exploring of that old building. There seemed little doubt that he was still in the cellar. The damp, tainted air which played coldly round his nostrils and the slimy feel of the floor beneath his fingers assured him of this. He wondered if his assailant after securing him had gone, or whether he was still somewhere in the house above, and for some minutes he listened intently to see if he could hear the slightest movement; but there was no sound. Everything was deathly still, except for the faint, rhythmic lap, lap of water, the same sound that he had heard when he had been standing in the scullery. Except for a more than usually painful headache and an unpleasant stiffness in his right shoulder, he was feeling practically his ordinary self. His brain was quite clear and alert, and he began to consider how best he could get out of this uncomfortable position.

The first thing, of course, was to free himself from these confounded ropes, and as a preliminary to this he began to test the knots. He soon found, however, that the person who had bound him had made an extremely good job of it. The knots refused to give a fraction of an inch, and the more he strained at them the tighter they became. His captor had also taken the precaution of thoroughly soaking the rope in water before using it — Peter could feel the wetness against his wrists — and he knew that as it dried it would become even tighter still.

He gave up his attempts at last and lay breathing a little heavily from his exertions and racking his brains to find some other way of getting out of this trap into which he had fallen. But he could think of nothing.

Presently as he lay there he heard a slight sound which he had not heard before. A gentle sibilant sound which was almost inaudible. The sound of somebody breathing close at hand! It came from somewhere quite near, and he concluded that he had only just heard it because before the faint lap, lap of the water had drowned it. Now, however, he had become used to that monotonous accompaniment.

He turned his head in the direction of the soft hissing and listened. Yes, there could be no doubt, somebody was there in the cellar with him, hidden by the pall of darkness. Who was it? The answer to his question flashed through his mind almost at the same instant as the question itself. John Lane!

'Who's that? Who's there?' he called softly into the blackness, but there was no reply.

There was, however, a slight alteration in the breathing. It stopped suddenly, paused and then went on jerkily. The person he had called to had heard him.

But why hadn't he replied? Obviously because he couldn't, and this suggested that, unlike Peter, he had been gagged as well as bound.

'Listen!' continued the reporter in the same low tone. 'If you can't speak, answer my questions by giving two sharp breaths for 'yes' and one longer one for 'no.' Do you understand?'

Two quick, sharp hisses answered him.

'Good!' said Peter. 'Are you John Lane?'

Again came the affirmative answer.

'Have you been here long?'

There came one long-drawn breath.

'Do you know who was responsible for bringing you here?'

Again one long breath answered him.

'Now, listen,' continued the reporter. 'I conclude that you are tied up pretty much the same as I am, but if you can move your fingers we may be able to help each other. Roll over towards me — you can judge the direction from the sound of my voice.'

There came a movement from the darkness, and after an interval Peter felt

238

someone bump up gently against him.

'Now,' he said, 'I'll move over on my side so that my hands, which are behind my back, are towards you. See if you can work yourself down until the knot that secures your gag is touching my fingers.'

The other began to shift his position, and presently Escott felt the back of a head press against his wrists.

'That's right,' he said. 'Keep there!'

He searched about with his fingers, and at length they came in contact with a hard, round object at the nape of the other's neck. It was the knot holding the gag in position. Peter set to work to untie it. It was a difficult job, but at last he managed it, and with aching fingers and broken nails pulled the gag from about John Lane's mouth.

'That's better,' he said in a husky whisper. 'Good heavens, my jaws ache! Who are you, and how did you get here?'

'Never mind that now,' said Peter. 'There will be plenty of time to ask and answer questions when we've succeeded in getting out of this place. At the present moment see if you can do the same with the knots at my wrists as I did with that gag. You ought to be able to manage it quite easily.'

'I'll do my best, anyhow,' said Lane, and hauled himself round until he could reach behind him and touch the ropes at Peter's wrists.

It was a much more difficult job than the untying of the gag, for Peter's endeavours to get free had only had the effect of tightening the knots, and in the wet condition of the rope this made them almost unshiftable. At the end of what the reporter considered must have been nearly twenty minutes Lane had scarcely succeeded in loosening them one iota, and then while he was still occupied in this task there came the sound of footsteps in the house above.

'Quick!' whispered Peter sharply. 'Get as far away from me as possible.'

Lane obeyed as best he could, and the footsteps which had drawn nearer stopped. There was the sound of a key turning in a lock, and then as the door at the top of the flight of rough steps opened the darkness fled before the yellow flame of a candle held in the hand of a man who stood on the threshold.

From where he lay Peter could see the newcomer. He was a thin man, dressed in a fawn-coloured macintosh, but he had taken the precaution of tying a handkerchief over the lower part of his face so that it was impossible to recognise him. He came down the stairs slowly, holding the candle above his head, and approached the bound figure of the reporter.

For a second or two he stood looking down at him in silence, and then he nodded slowly.

'Recovered your senses, have you?' he said in a voice that was rough and uncultured. 'Well, that's darned unlucky for you!'

Peter made no reply, and the man without speaking again moved over and stuck the candle on a brick-work ledge. Peter wondered whether he would notice the fact that John Lane was without the gag, but glancing out of the corner of his eye, he saw that Lane had succeeded in rolling himself into a far corner of the cellar, and was so obscured by shadow as to be almost invisible. He hoped fervently that the new-comer would not examine him too closely, and apparently the other had no intention of doing so, for having secured the candle with a splash of wax to the ledge he proceeded to unload his pockets of the various articles with which they were bulging.

Peter watched him with growing surprise. First of all he produced a chisel, followed by a short crowbar, and then a thing that looked like a marline-spike, only that it was longer and thinner. He laid these on the floor under the light of the candle, and then, going over to the wall at right angles to the flight of steps, he began to examine it carefully. He took a long time over this, but at last he apparently found what he wanted, for having stooped down and peered at a spot about a foot above the ground, he gave a little grunt of satisfaction, and came back to the place where he had laid out the instruments.

Still wondering what all this portended,

Peter continued to watch him interestedly. He selected the object that looked like a marline-spike and returning with this to the wall which he had been examining, squatted down on his haunches and with the sharp point of the instrument began to pick at the brick-work.

Chip, chip, chip. Chip, chip, chip! The noise he made was barely audible, and Peter concluded from this that he was working on the mortar between the bricks. The reporter tried to guess what he was up to, for it seemed a singularly senseless proceeding, and then like a flash the explanation occurred to him and his heart went cold.

The man continued to work steadily and methodically. He finished using the marline-spike and came over for the crowbar, and looking at the place where he had been working, Peter saw that he had succeeded in removing all the mortar from around one brick. Yes, the horrible idea that had entered his mind was correct. There was no doubt of it.

The man in the macintosh returned

with the crowbar and inserting it in the interstice he had made, began to wrench at the brick. It came away in small pieces at first, but presently, as he got more purchase with the crowbar, they became larger until the entire brick had been removed. And now the gentle lap, lap of water, which had kept up a running accompaniment all the time the reporter had been in the cellar, grew louder and into the musty, evil-smelling air came a draught of cold, river-scented breeze.

The man in the macintosh flung down the crowbar that he had been using, and crossing to the candle picked it up and came over to Peter.

'I see you've been watching me,' he said sneeringly, 'and I've no doubt that clever brain of yours has tumbled to what I've been up to. In case you haven't I might as well tell you before I go. I dare say when you were spying round this place you noticed that the back of this house is almost flush with the river. If you didn't notice it before, I'm telling you now. As a matter of fact, only a narrow broken-down wharf separates it, and that only separates the upper part and the back door. This cellar is built out under the wharf, and that wall which I've been experimenting with is the outside wall, and there's nothing beyond it but the river. At the present moment it's low tide and you're getting a nice lot of healthy air, but at high tide the water comes up nearly to the level of the wharf, which means that it's above the roof of this cellar. Since I've made the hole in that wall I don't think there's any need for me to tell you what's going to happen. I was reserving this for that fellow over there,' he jerked his head in the direction of Lane, 'but since you would poke your nose into other people's business you may as well share what was coming to him. I've got one more thing to do before I leave you.'

He set the candle down, and taking a handkerchief from his pocket stooped and bound it about the reporter's mouth.

'That's just in case your shouting attracts anybody's attention,' he said, straightening up. 'I don't suppose they'd hear it, but there's just a chance they might now that brick's out. Anyway, it won't be long before the water covers it, and then you could shout as much as you like. The tide's on the turn now. Has been for the last half hour, so you won't have long to wait!'

He picked up the candle and without another word went up the wooden steps and passed through the door at the top. It closed gently behind him and the key turned. Peter heard the sound of his steps retreating in the distance, and then silence once more settled down over the building.

'What are we going to do now?' John Lane's voice, husky and faint, floated out of the darkness.

Peter grunted. It was all he could do, and he heard a slithering, scraping sound as the other dragged and rolled himself towards him.

'I'll try and see if I can't get that gag off,' Lane whispered in his ear, and after a little while Peter felt him fiddling with the knot at the back of his head.

The man must have tied it carelessly,

for in a very short time he felt it loosen, and shook it clear of his mouth.

'Thanks,' he said. 'Now the best thing to do is to shout and see if we can't attract somebody's attention from outside.'

'I don't think I shall be much good at shouting,' said Lane hoarsely. 'I've had nothing to eat or drink since I was brought here, and my throat is like a rasp. Anyhow, I'll do my best.'

They shouted, and the sound of their voices boomed round the confining walls of the cellar, but Peter doubted very much whether they would penetrate sufficiently to attract the attention of anyone outside. They shouted until they were hoarse, and then lay gasping and panting, and in the silence that followed an ominous sound reached the reporter's ears. Mingled with the lap, lap of the water outside was a steady trickling. The river had already begun to enter the cellar.

'There's only one thing for it,' he said to Lane. 'We've got to get free from these confounded ropes. You weren't very successful with me; let me see if I can't be more successful with you.'

He twisted about until he was able to work on the knots at Lane's wrists, and at these he tugged and pulled, trying vainly to loosen them. But it was difficult working by sense of touch alone, and although he tore his fingers he made no impression on the other's bonds. A cold sensation along one side of his body warned him that the water was already spreading over the floor of the cellar, and pausing in his labours for a moment to listen he discovered that the gentle trickle had grown into a steady rush! Another fifteen minutes he reckoned would see the water above their heads. He redoubled his efforts until the warm blood from his broken nails was trickling over his palms, but the knots refused to yield. Lane in his struggles to loosen them had done the same as Peter had done; made them so tight that the reporter doubted that anything short of a knife would be of any avail.

The water, too, was now hampering him, for it had risen to the level of his chin. He gave up his attempts at last with an exclamation of despair.

'I'm afraid it's useless, Lane,' he gasped. 'I can't do anything with those ropes.'

'But good God!' cried Lane, in a thin reedy whisper. 'We must do something! If we don't, in another minute or two, we shall be drowned like rats in a trap!'

19

Mr. Ginnings Takes a Hand

'And wot,' said Mr. Ginnings, eyeing his plate with a gloomy aversion, 'the 'ell do you call this 'ere?'

His wife stopped in the act of pouring water from a steaming kettle into the teapot and looked across the kitchen.

'An 'addock,' she said briefly.

'An 'addock?' repeated Mr. Ginnings scornfully. 'An' 'ow long ago was it an 'addock, that's wot I'd like to know.'

'What's the matter with it?' she demanded.

'Matter with it?' echoed her husband, digging the unfortunate fish viciously with a knife. 'Old age, that's wot's the matter with it. Where did yer get it?'

'Purvis's,' said Mrs. Ginnings, finishing making the tea and bringing the pot over to the table.

'Well, don't get no more at Purvis's,'

said her husband. 'This ain't the first time
'e's done it on yer. An 'addock,' he
muttered below his breath.

'Oh, yer always grumblin' at your food,'
she said. 'Sinful I calls it. Temptin'
Providence, that's what it is.'

'Temptin' Providence,' repeated Mr.
Ginnings. He had a habit of repeating all
his wife's last remarks in order to give
himself time to think out a crushing
retort. 'You couldn't tempt no one with
this 'ere fish.'

'Well, it can't be so bad,' said Mrs.
Ginnings. 'Alf 'ad some of it for 'is tea,
and he said nothin' about it. That fish yer
'ad was all right, wasn't it, Alf?'

She appealed to a thin, weedy youth
who was busily engaged at the dresser
with his head buried in an oblong box.

'Eh?' said Alf in a muffled voice
without removing his head from this
contraption. 'Wot'cher say?'

'That 'addock ye had for tea was all
right, wasn't it?'

'Short circuit somewhere,' muttered
Alf. 'Wot'cher say?'

Mrs. Ginnings repeated her remark in a

voice that must have been audible half a mile away.

'I didn't notice nothin' wrong,' said Alf, temporarily withdrawing his head from the box. 'Why?'

''cos your father's grumblin',' said his mother.

'An' ain't I got cause to grumble?' snorted Mr. Ginnings with righteous indignation. ''ere am I an 'ard workin' man what comes 'ome lookin' forward to 'is bit o' grub, an' this is what I gets. An 'addock wot they must 'ave dug up to see what it died of!'

'Oh, give it to me!' said the lady of the house, 'an' for 'eaven's sake stop grumblin'. 'ere you are. Drink yer tea, while I goes and cooks yer some eggs.'

'Ain't yer got nothin' else?' demanded her husband.

'No I ain't,' said Mrs. Ginnings. 'If yer don't want them, yer'll 'ave to eat the 'addock or go without altogether.'

She picked up the plate and disappeared into the scullery.

'Nice thin',' said Mr. Ginnings, addressing nobody in particular. 'A *nice* thin' for an 'ard workin' man!'

He seemed to like this phrase, for he repeated it several times below his breath.

An appalling squeal followed by several crackles and a series of grunts emanated from the box on the dresser over which Alf was bending, and Mr. Ginnings started. 'Wot the 'ell is that?' he asked crossly.

Alf looked round with a flushed face. 'Berlin!' he said proudly.

'Is it?' said Mr. Ginnings darkly. 'Well you switch the darn thing on to something else. Don't make any more of that row, d'yer 'ear, or I'll clip you round your ear 'ole.'

'You leave the boy alone!' cried a voice from the scullery. 'Let 'im do 'is wireless if 'e wants to. 'e ain't interferin' with you.'

'Look 'ere!' roared Mr. Ginnings. 'Am I the boss of this 'ere 'ouse, or am I not?'

'Not!' snapped his wife succinctly, and the reply so astonished Mr. Ginnings that he glared at the scullery door, momentarily bereft of speech.

'What 'ave you been doin' to-day to make you so bad-tempered?' said Mrs.

Ginnings, hurrying in and beginning to cut large, thick slices of bread and butter. 'Bin in the Crown an' Anchor, I suppose. Beer always did upset yer.'

'That's right!' snarled her husband. 'Go on, 'cuse me of bein' drunk just 'cos I won't eat an 'addock which ain't fit to put on a dust 'eap. Just like ye, it is! Take after yer mother, yer do!'

'You leave my mother alone!' said Mrs. Ginnings angrily.

'Wouldn't touch 'er with a barge pole, the old cat!' declared Mr. Ginnings feelingly.

His wife laid down the knife with which she had been buttering the bread, and placing both hands on her hips, surveyed her husband with enraged eyes.

'Bert Ginnings,' she said, 'you just be careful what yer sayin'!'

Mr. Ginnings opened his mouth to reply, when Alf intervened with a dreadful rising howl from the wireless set.

'Don't seem right some'ow,' he said shaking his head. 'Don't think it ought to do.'

'Drat the boy!' cried Mrs. Ginnings.

'We'll 'ave the neighbours complainin' if 'e goes on like that!'

'Well you encourages 'im,' said her husband crossly. 'Leave the thin' alone, Alf, do yer 'ear!'

'I'm tryin' to get Berlin,' said Alf in an injured voice.

'Well don't try no more. We don't want it. 'sides it ain't patriotic,' growled his father. ''ere's people tellin' you to buy British, and you go tryin' to get Berlin. I'm ashamed of you!'

'You're a good one to be ashamed of anybody,' said Mrs. Ginnings, resuming her buttering operations. 'If instead of talkin' so much yer'd make yerself a bit useful it would be better for all of us.'

'What d'ye want now?' said her husband.

'Coal,' said his wife. 'The fire'll be out in a minute, an' the scuttle's empty.'

Mr. Ginnings rose to his feet, and hitched up his trousers with a sigh of resignation. 'Suppose I've got to go and fill it,' he grunted. 'Nice thin' for an 'ard workin' man what looks forward to a bit of rest in the evenin'!'

He crossed over to the fireplace and picked up the scuttle. 'Where's the candle?' he demanded.

'Where it always is,' answered his wife. 'On the copper.'

Keeping up a low muttering in which the words ''ard workin' man' could just be distinguished, Mr. Ginnings carried the scuttle out into the scullery and lit the candle. Presently his wife heard a smothered exclamation, and then his voice called her urgently. She hurried out into the scullery, and found her husband standing half-way down the wooden steps that led into the cellar. He was holding the candle high above his head, and when she reached his side, she saw that he was staring at several inches of water that covered the cellar floor.

'Good 'eavens!' she said. ''ow on earth did that get there?'

'Pipe must have bust or somethin',' said Mr. Ginnings. 'There's always somethin' wrong in this bloomin' 'ouse. If it ain't — '

He broke off as his wife clutched his arm suddenly.

'Wot'cher doin'?' he exclaimed crossly. 'You nearly pitched me off these 'ere steps!'

'Did yer 'ear it?' she whispered.

'Did I 'ear what?' he demanded.

'That noise,' she said excitedly, 'like somebody callin' out!'

Mr. Ginnings looked at her with disfavour. 'You taken to 'earin' things now?' he asked.

''oo would be callin' out?'

'I don't know, but I 'eared it,' said his wife. 'Like a cry for 'elp it was. Seemed as if it came from the other side of that wall.'

'Wot shows you're talkin' nonsense,' said Mr. Ginnings. 'The other side of that there wall is the empty 'ouse.'

She looked at him queerly. 'Yes I know,' she said. 'But there's been somethin' funny goin' on there lately. Only the other night when you was out, I thought I 'eard somebody movin' about in there, and now — Hark! There it is again.'

This time Mr. Ginnings heard it himself: A faint muffled cry that came from the other side of the cellar wall.

'There *is* someone in there all right!' he

exclaimed quickly, 'an' they're in trouble too, by the sound of it. I'm goin' to see what's 'appenin'.'

He pushed past his wife and re-entered the scullery.

''ere, Alf, come an' give us a 'and,' he roared as he put down the candle, and began unbolting the back door.

The weedy youth joined him.

'Wot'cher goin' to do, Bert?' asked Mrs. Ginnings, breathless with excitement.

'I'm goin' to see what's goin' on in the cellar next door,' he declared, pulling open the back door and going out into the darkness of the night. 'Come on, Alf!'

The back exit of Mr. Ginnings's house led into a small yard, oblong in shape, and divided from the other houses by low wooden fences. At the end of this yard was a stone wall which separated it from the river, a little more than eight feet distant from the house itself. Mr. Ginnings, followed by his lanky son, proceeded to climb the intervening fence into the yard belonging to the empty house next door. He made for the back door and tried the handle, but it was shut and fastened and refused to give when he shook it.

'Ain't no good tryin' that way,' he muttered. 'Perhaps we'll 'ave better luck with the winder.'

The window at the side of the door was composed of six small panes of glass, and Mr. Ginnings, inserting his fingers under the sash, tried to raise it. It refused to budge.

'It's latched, I 'spect,' said Alf helpfully.

His father took out a soiled handkerchief, wrapped it round his knuckles, and with one blow smashed a pane of glass which was directly under where the catch would be. Putting his hand through the jagged hole he felt about and pushed back the catch. A further attempt resulted in the window opening to the accompaniment of a loud screeching noise. Mr. Ginnings hoisted himself across the sill, and dropped into the scullery beyond. Turning, he helped his son to scramble through the window after him, and then striking a match he looked about. As he did so, more clearly now and less muffled, came the cry for help. It came from behind the closed door leading to the cellar.

'There's somebody down there,' said Mr. Ginnings, while his son, with open mouth and bulging eyes, stared fascinated at the door. His father crossed the scullery, and tugged at the handle. The door was locked and here Mr. Ginnings proved himself to be a man of resource. Dropping the match which was burning his fingers, he handed the box to his son, and without hesitation hurled himself against the door. At the third onslaught the lock gave with a splintering crash and the door flew open. Mr. Ginnings stumbled forward and brought up heavily against the opposite wall, only saving himself from falling headlong down the steps by clutching wildly at the jamb of the door.

'Hurry! For God's sake hurry!' croaked a voice from the darkness below, and snatching the matchbox from his son's hand, Mr. Ginnings struck a match and peered down the steps.

A smooth lake of water met his gaze,

lapping the lower steps, and just raised an inch above the dark surface two white faces that glimmered dimly in the yellow flame from the match. Mr. Ginnings uttered a lurid expletive.

'Well, I'll be — !' he ejaculated. ''ere's a go!' And at that moment the match he was holding went out.

20

John Lane Explains

Peter Escott stretched out his feet to the cosy warmth of the gas fire in his sitting-room and inhaled the smoke from his cigarette gratefully.

'That's more comfortable,' he remarked. 'I don't think I shall forget to-night very easily.'

John Lane, a rather grotesque-looking figure in one of the reporter's suits, which was much too big for him, nodded in agreement.

'I don't think I shall ever forget it,' he declared. 'Those last few minutes seemed an eternity.'

'We ought to be very thankful to the gas company,' said Peter. 'If their pipes hadn't been laid through the intervening walls, the water would never have penetrated into the cellar of the adjoining house, and we should probably have been drowned by now.'

'But if there was an outlet,' said Mr. Trimmer from the depths of an armchair, 'that ought to have stopped the water rising high enough to do any damage.'

'It would,' said the reporter, 'if it hadn't been coming in faster than it went out. As it was, it delayed matters long enough to enable Mr. Ginnings to appear on the scene just in time. Another minute and he would have been too late.'

Peter was not exaggerating. When the man from next door had found them it had been touch and go. But after his first glimpse of those white faces almost level with the water, he and his son had acted promptly, and had succeeded in dragging them to safety. He had been intensely curious to know how they had got into that unpleasant position, and his curiosity had reached fever point when he saw that their wrists and ankles were bound. It was only with the greatest difficulty that Peter had prevented his rushing off immediately for the nearest policeman, for the man seemed to have got it firmly fixed in his mind that they were a pair of desperate criminals and that it was his duty to see that they were instantly locked up. The opportune arrival, however, of Mr. Trimmer with a sergeant in a police car had prevented this happening. Peter had been intensely surprised to see his friend, and in answer to his question, Mr. Trimmer smiled rather dolefully.

'You weren't the only person who noticed that white tar,' he said. 'But I thought if it amused you to think so, I'd let you! We were just comin' to examine the house.'

He made a hasty search of the place, while Peter and John Lane shivered in front of Mrs. Ginnings's kitchen fire, without finding anything, and then he drove them back to Peter's flat in the police car. They arrived chilled to the bone, but a rub-down and a change of clothes soon put them right, and seated in front of the sitting-room fire Peter had told the interested inspector his adventures.

'Now,' said Mr. Trimmer, looking across at John Lane a little wearily, 'I should like to hear exactly what happened to you.'

'That won't take very long,' answered Lane. 'I'd been in all the evening. As a matter of fact, I spent it making a list of the money I owed to various people and trying to think out some scheme by which I could keep the more pressing of them quiet.' He smiled ruefully. 'It wasn't a very pleasant occupation, or very successful. In the end I gave it up, and was just thinking of going to bed, when the bell rang. It was getting late, and I wondered who the deuce it could be at that hour. I knew of nobody who was likely to call on me; the only people who ever came as a rule were people I owed money to and men with summonses, and it was too late for either of these. At first I thought I would let them go on ringing until they got tired and went away, but whoever it was was so persistent that I eventually decided to see what it was all about. It struck me that it might possibly be a message from my uncle.'

'Didn't you know that he was dead?' put in Peter.

Lane shook his head. 'No,' he replied. 'I hadn't seen a paper for several days, and

I'd heard nothing. I went down and opened the main door, and found a fellow standing on the step, the same fellow who nearly succeeded in putting an end to us in that cellar to-night.'

'Can you describe him?' asked Mr. Trimmer.

'Only vaguely,' said Lane. He gave a rough description, and it tallied almost exactly with that of the man who had hired the car from Mr. Shipman. 'I asked him what he wanted,' continued Lane, 'and he said that he had come from Miss Margaret Maddox. He said that she wanted to see me urgently at Maddox Court in connection with the murder. This was the first I had heard of any murder, and I asked him what he meant. He seemed surprised that I didn't know all about it, and told me that my uncle had been found dead in his study, and that the police were holding the man who had done it. Naturally I was amazed and horrified. He said that he didn't know what my cousin wanted me for, but that she had sent a car to take me back. I asked him to come in while I had a wash and got my hat and coat. He agreed and we went upstairs to the flat. I showed him into the sitting-room, gave him a cigarette and asked him to wait a moment. I was washing my hands in the bedroom when something wet was pressed over my nose and mouth, and I don't remember anything more until I woke up and found myself in that confounded cellar.'

'You didn't pack a bag to take with you to Maddox Court?' asked the chief inspector mournfully.

'No,' answered the other wonderingly. 'Why?'

'Your suitcase was missing, an' a lot of your things had gone out of the drawers,' answered Mr. Trimmer. 'That was done, of course, to make it look as though you'd gone away of your own free will.'

'I don't see with what object,' grunted Lane.

'It's plain enough,' Mr. Trimmer sighed. 'Your uncle had been murdered, an' it was fairly common knowledge that you had quarrelled with him. You were in difficulties over money, an' by his death you stood to inherit five thousand pounds. Naturally, suspicion would rest on you.'

'By Jove, you mean that it was a plot?' exclaimed Lane. 'To try and involve me in my uncle's death?'

'I don't think there's much doubt of it,' grunted the inspector. 'Findin' that their first victim was likely to slip out of the net in which they had entangled him, these people wanted to find somebody else to take his place.'

'Their first victim?' repeated Lane. 'Whom are you talking about?'

Peter told him about Dick Mason.

'But who are these people?' asked Lane when the reporter had finished.

Peter shook his head. 'At the present moment we don't know,' he said. 'I've a suspicion that Hake is mixed up in the business, but who the others are, if there are any others, I don't know.'

'All we do know,' said Mr. Trimmer, 'is that there must be a very strong motive at the back of it. For three people have already been killed, not counting the attempt on your lives to-night.'

Lane looked at him, aghast. 'Three

268

people?' he cried. 'You don't mean to say that there have been other murders besides my uncle?'

'Tell him all about it, Peter,' said the chief inspector, leaning back in his chair and closing his eyes.

Peter did so, and John Lane listened attentively. When he had concluded he whistled softly.

'It's astounding!' he said, 'and as complete a mystery to me as apparently it is to you. Of course, I knew Annie Berman. We all did; she was rather a family institution. But why anybody should want to kill her, is beyond me.'

'It's beyond me, too, at the moment,' admitted Peter. 'Except that I believe she was killed because she knew too much. How long have Hake, Rand & Hake handled your uncle's affairs?'

'As long as I can remember,' said Lane. 'That's why it makes it so difficult for me to imagine that Hake can have anything to do with these crimes. Why, I've known him since I was a little boy.'

'There isn't a criminal in the world,' said Mr. Trimmer, opening his eyes for a moment, 'who somebody hasn't known since they were a little boy. It's a stupid thin' to think that the people we knew in childhood all have haloes.'

'I suppose you're right to a certain extent,' admitted Lane. 'But it's difficult to think of old Hake as a murderer.'

'Nobody's sayin' that he is,' grunted the inspector. 'But there's somethin' fishy about him all the same. My present difficulty is to fix him with a motive. Peter's idea is that he's been dippin' rather freely into Sir James' fortune. But I can't see how the murder would help him to cover up that. It 'ud be more likely to have the opposite effect.'

'Not,' said Peter, 'if Sir James's financial affairs were so arranged that the investment of his money was entirely in Hake's hands. In that case, with Sir James out of the way, Hake would be in a pretty strong position. It would be next to impossible to check any statement that he might make, and it would be quite easy for him to cover up any embezzlement he may have committed.'

'The only way to find out for certain,'

said Mr. Trimmer, sitting up and glancing at his watch, 'is to get Miss Maddox's permission, an' authority to have her father's affairs looked into by a competent accountant. I'm goin' back to the Yard now,' he said, rising to his feet. 'I've got some work to do. If you like,' he looked at John Lane, 'I'll drop you at the Bently Buildings.'

Lane thanked him, and saying good night to Peter, went off with the inspector.

Peter sat smoking for some time before he went to bed, and then finding that he was dropping into a doze, he went into his bedroom and undressing quickly slipped between the sheets. He fell asleep almost as soon as his head touched the pillow, and he slept dreamlessly until the jangle of his alarm clock brought him back to wakefulness and the beginning of another day.

21

Broken Glass!

Peter woke feeling a little irritable, and this increased as the morning wore on. Mr. Stevens, the news editor, was not in the best of tempers that morning — even news editors have their domestic troubles — and was inclined to be annoyed that the big story Peter had hinted at was not forthcoming.

'So far we've printed nothing about the Maddox case that hasn't appeared in every other newspaper,' he grumbled. 'You'd better get a move on.'

This didn't tend to make Peter feel any brighter, and neither did his telephone conversation with Chief Inspector Trimmer shortly after. The reports had come through from the men who had been put on to enquire into the movements of Mr. Hake on the night of the murder, and the lawyer was provided with an almost unshakable alibi. He had arrived home from his office shortly after seven, and after his dinner had complained of feeling unwell. He had apparently had a slight temperature, and the doctor who had been sent for ordered him to bed at once, and there he had stayed until the following morning. There were at least three people who were prepared to swear to this: the butler, the housemaid who had carried up a light supper at eleven, and the cook who had prepared this supper. There was not the slightest doubt that at the time when the murder had been committed at Maddox Court, Mr. Hake was in bed in his bedroom, in his house at Sydenham. He could, therefore, have had no actual hand in the crime. But this did not preclude the possibility that he had planned it. Somebody else, working under his orders, might have actually carried it out. Peter thought this was more than likely, and said so, and Mr. Trimmer agreed with him. It was going to be difficult, however, under the circumstances, to prove Hake's connection with the murderer at all. There was nothing like sufficient evidence to warrant arresting the man, and however suspicious the police might be concerning him, they could do nothing.

Things seemed to have arrived at a deadlock. So far as Peter could see the only way of implicating the lawyer was to find his accomplice, and this was by no means easy. The accomplice, or one of them at any rate, was obviously the man in the soiled macintosh, but unfortunately neither Mr. Shipman nor John Lane could give a sufficiently clear description of him to make it the slightest use. There were hundreds of men walking about the streets of London whom their somewhat vague description would fit. Peter was pretty sure that this man was the same man who had offered Dick Mason the ten pounds to carry the fake letter to Maddox Court. But the difficulty was to find him. Taking all things into consideration, his ill temper was not to be wondered at.

Halfway through the afternoon he made up his mind to go to Maddox Court and see Margaret Maddox, in the hope that he could learn something from her. He put a telephone call through in order to let her know that he was coming, but Gilder, who answered, said that the girl was out for a walk and was not expected back until tea-time. He left a message for the butler to give her, and leaving the *Megaphone* offices, got into his car. In the meantime, as there was no object in his reaching Maddox Court before the girl came home, he decided to drop in and see Frank Lane. He sent the little car humming along Fleet Street in the direction of that gentleman's residence, and reached the big block of flats just before four. But here luck was against him. The same manservant opened the door, and in reply to his enquiry informed him that Mr. Lane had gone out of town for a few days.

'He's gone to Maddox Court, sir,' said the man. 'I don't know whether I'm doing wrong in telling you that, but seeing as you're one of the gentlemen engaged in clearing up the matter of his uncle's death, I suppose it's all right.'

'When did he leave?' asked Peter, and the servant told him that his master had left that morning.

The reporter thanked him, and made his way back to the car. He wondered just why Mr. Lane had gone to High Wycombe, and concluded that most probably it was to talk over some business arrangement with his cousin. It did not matter very much, anyway; he would have a chance of speaking to him when he got there himself.

He backed the car, turned it round, and set off for High Wycombe, never dreaming that Fate decreed that he was not to reach his destination. He stopped halfway on his journey for a cup of tea, and by the time he had started again dusk was falling, and it had come on to rain. The road from High Wycombe to Maddox Court ran through a thick wood, sloping down to a copse of trees, and rising up to the crest of a hill on the other side. As the car sped down among the trees, the twilight deepened to a midnight gloom. Peter was just thinking what an unpleasantly lonely place it was when there was a loud report and the car swerved violently.

'Damn it!' he muttered, 'that's a tyre gone!'

He pressed hard on the clutch pedal, and wrenched hard at the hand brake. As the car came to a halt he jumped out, and bending down looked at the wheels. The right-hand back tyre was as flat as a pancake, and he uttered a little exclamation of exasperation. There was nothing for it but to put on the spare wheel, and opening the tool box underneath the seat, he searched for the jack. Hauling this out he put it down by the back of the car, and went round to the other side to unstrap the spare wheel. His fingers were at work on the straps when he saw something, and his face set grimly. The tyre had been slashed! A deep cut extended for nearly four inches. Peter frowned and a tingle of excitement ran through him. The bursting of the back tyre had not been an accident; he had been meant to stop here.

He looked about him a little uneasily. He was at the bottom of a dip in a small valley-like depression of the road, where the trees and undergrowth grew close about him, and formed thick, impenetrable screens. His eyes searched the darkness and he listened, but only the rustling of the branches in the slight wind came to his ears. If amid the darkness of those thickly-clustered trunks a danger lurked, it was a silent danger. He felt the hair stir a little on the back of his neck, but he shook off the momentary fear that had gripped him, and pulling out his pocket torch walked slowly back a few yards along the way he had come, shining the light on the road. Presently he saw something glisten, and stopped. A closer examination showed him that the surface of the road at this point had been strewn with broken glass. So that was the cause of the burst tyre.

He went back to the car, flashing the torch on the thickly growing trees on either side as he walked. The rain was coming down heavily now, and to his imagination it seemed as if the darkness had eyes that were watching him, and the rustle of the drops on the fallen leaves was like the soft patter of stealthy footsteps. But he saw nothing. And yet these elaborate preparations must have some serious object behind them. Someone must have followed him from his flat, and slashed the spare tyre when he stopped for tea. His lips curled back into a grin that had no vestige of mirth in it. Had all this trouble been taken just to delay his arrival at Maddox Court, or was there something infinitely more sinister behind it? If there was, they couldn't have chosen a better place.

He reached the car, and switching out the torch took a revolver from one of the door pockets. It was an old weapon but it was loaded and might prove useful. It struck him that the most sensible thing he could do would be to abandon the crippled car, and go back to High Wycombe, but there was a stubborn streak in Peter's nature; besides which he was intensely curious to know the reason for his having been forced to stop at this particular spot. Something had been planned to happen, and he wanted to know exactly what that something was.

Two minutes later he did!

22

Vanished!

Inspector Burnett sat at the desk in his little office and stared rather gloomily at the blotting pad. He was not feeling at all cheerful, for he had that afternoon had an interview with Major Hilling, the chief constable, during the course of which that gentleman, after hearing all that the inspector had to say, had strongly advised the calling in of Scotland Yard.

'You may have got the right man, Burnett, in this fellow Mason,' he concluded. 'But you don't seem any too certain about it yourself. And anyway the evidence isn't conclusive enough to bring him up before a magistrate. The thing looked easy enough at the beginning, but now it's getting complicated, deuced complicated.'

The inspector had been forced to agree with him. It was complicated, much too complicated to please him, and yet he was reluctant to let it pass out of his hands. It would mean a big thing for him, if he could bring it to a successful conclusion, and Inspector Burnett had ambitions. He had asked the chief constable to hold over calling in the Yard for another three days, and behind his request lay the hope that Peter might by that time have some further news for him. Burnett was putting a lot of faith in the reporter; he had a flair for nosing out the truth in these sorts of cases. What was worrying the inspector was the other end of the case. The killing of Sneath had automatically brought the Yard into it, and he was desperately afraid that they might, during their investigation of the little nose's death, find the murderer of Sir James Maddox before he could. He was still holding on to Dick Mason, but he was by no means certain that he had got the right man; in fact he was pretty sure that he had not. And that was another thing that troubled him; he couldn't detain Mason indefinitely. He'd either have to formally charge him or let him go, and at the moment he wasn't in the position to do either.

He was still racking his brains when he heard the sound of heavy steps crossing the charge room, and the voice of Police Constable Wipple enquiring of the desk sergeant if he was in. He heard the sergeant's mumbled reply, and then there came a tap at the door, and it opened to admit the rather breathless figure of the policeman.

'What's the matter?' asked Burnett sharply as he caught sight of the other's face.

'I don't quite know, sir.' The constable was panting heavily and spoke with difficulty. 'But I've just found Mr. Escott's car in that dip by Merton's Wood. It's standing in the middle of the road and there's nobody with it.'

The inspector came quickly to his feet. 'What do you mean, there's nobody with it?' he demanded.

Wipple explained. He had been patrolling that part of the road when he had come upon the car. The lights were on but there was no sign of any driver or other occupant. He had examined the car, and discovered that one of the back tyres was flat, and that the spare tyre had been badly cut. A little farther along the road, he had come upon a lot of broken glass. He had recognised the car as belonging to Mr. Escott, and he had called several times, but had got no reply. He thought something had happened, and he had hurried to the station as quickly as possible to report the matter.

'You did quite right,' said Burnett. 'Wait here a minute and I'll be back.'

He put on his hat and coat and hurried round to the garage where he kept his car, and returning to the station with it picked up Wipple and drove towards Merton's Wood.

'I don't like the sound of it at all,' he said as they sped along. 'That broken glass and cut tyre look as if the whole thing had been premeditated.'

'That's what I thought, sir,' said the constable. 'Look, there's the car, sir.'

They had reached the crest of the hill, and he pointed to the headlights, and the dark outline below. Burnett grunted.

'H'm! The loneliest spot in the whole road,' he said.

'Mind the glass, sir,' said the constable. 'We're just on it now.'

Burnett nodded, and pulled up with a jerk. He jumped out and followed by the constable made his way towards the standing car. It was empty and deserted and there was no sign of life anywhere near at hand. Burnett looked uneasily at the policeman.

'Funny; where can he have gone to?' he remarked.

'Perhaps he went in search of help, sir,' suggested the constable, but the inspector shook his head. 'If he'd gone to the garage, I'd have seen something of him,' he answered. 'It's more probable that he was on his way to Maddox Court when this happened and decided to walk the rest of the way.' He looked about him quickly, and listened, but there was no sound except the dripping of the branches, and the faint whistle of a train in the distance.

'Well, he isn't anywhere around, that's a cert,' said the constable; he broke off staring at the ground, and Burnett swung round.

'What is it?' he said. 'What have you found?'

'Look!' Wipple's voice was hushed, as he stretched out his hand and pointed. 'Look there, sir!'

The inspector bent down and his heart went cold as he saw the glistening patch of red that mingled with the wet surface of the road.

'Blood!' he muttered. 'This looks bad. Something serious has happened,' and then he saw what he had not noticed before: two splintered holes in the woodwork of the car. 'Those are bullet holes,' he said. 'There's been shooting.'

The holes were in the side of the car, which was nearest to a thick screen of undergrowth.

'We'd better make a search, sir,' suggested Wipple, and although he didn't say what for, Burnett knew.

They spent a quarter of an hour, plunging among the undergrowth at the fringe of the wood, but they found nothing. Except for those two holes in the bodywork of the car, and the ominous stain, there was no sign of the tragedy that the inspector was certain now had been enacted in that lonely spot.

'There's only one thing to do,' he said, emerging from a tangled thicket, his face and hands scratched and torn from the thorns. 'We must have help. Men and lights. Go back to the station — ' He tore a sheet from his notebook and bending before the car lights, wrote rapidly — 'and take this to Sergeant Lee.'

Wipple nodded, and going back to the police car, started the engine with a roar. It moved off, and Burnett watched the red star of the tail lamp fade up the hill. He waited in the silence that followed, and although he was not a particularly imaginative man, he could picture the solitary figure of the reporter by the side of the useless car, helpless to defend himself from the fate that had overtaken him. But what was it that had happened? A shot from the darkness of the wood? A slumping figure that fell forward on to the sodden surface of the road leaving behind that ominous stain of blood? Burnett shivered; the picture was all too vivid for comfort. Somewhere near at hand someone might still be lurking, waiting for a further victim. It was not a pleasant thought, and he moved nearer to the car until his back was against it, watching with intent eyes the shadowy masses of the wood. The ordinary darkness of a moonless night had succeeded the gloom of the rain-clouds, and overhead the stars twinkled brightly.

Presently, there came the low hum of a car, and he saw the lights of it rushing towards him down the hill. It drew up with a jerk and Sergeant Lee, Wipple and three more policemen got out and came over to the inspector. Burnett began rapping out orders, and twinkling lights like giant glow-worms started to flit hither and thither among the gaunt trunks of the trees. The inspector joined in with a heavy heart, waiting for the call from one of the party that would herald the discovery he feared. But it never came. The dawn gradually turned the darkness to light, and then the sun rose and flooded the countryside with pale yellow, and still the search went on.

It was high in the heavens when the last yard of wooded land had been combed, but nothing had been found. Peter Escott had vanished as completely and utterly as though absorbed in the darkness of that rainy night.

23

Betty Learns the Truth

Betty Hardy woke to the sound of the shrill burring of the alarm clock that stood on the little table beside her bed. In that dazed condition which precedes full wakefulness she stretched out an arm and turned off the noisy harbinger of the coming day. She lay for a few seconds staring at the ceiling, and then, resisting a strong inclination to go to sleep again, slipped out of bed and, pulling a dressing-gown round her, went into the little kitchenette and put the kettle on for her breakfast. While it was boiling she had her bath and dressed, and then came back and made the tea.

She occupied a very tiny flat in Grayling Street, a turning near Southampton Row. It was even smaller than Peter's, but to her it was home, and was a hundred per cent better than the tenement she had lived in during her childhood.

Betty ate her breakfast slowly, with her thoughts fixed on Dick and his terrible position. Not that she was as worried as she had been. Peter Escott had given her confidence. There was something about his strong personality that spelt success and negated all ideas of failure. He believed that Dick was innocent, and sooner or later he would prove it. She was sure of that.

Her mind switched from that to the taunt flung at her by the drunken Mrs. Berman. Was it true? Had her father been hanged for murder? She had only the vaguest recollection of her childhood and the woman whom she had been taught to call 'Auntie': a hard-faced, heavy-handed creature of whom she had gone in terror. She remembered the miserable house in Rose Water Lane, Battersea, and her uncle, a man who was always out of work and continually quarrelling with her aunt. She remembered the day when the woman had been taken ill and retired to a bed from which she was never destined to rise. But she had no recollection at all of either of her parents. They must have died before she was old enough to realise things. So occupied was she with her thoughts that the time slipped by without her being aware of its swiftness, and it was nearly nine o'clock when she rose hastily and put on her hat and coat.

Mr. Hake was a stickler for punctuality. One of the greatest crimes in his eyes was to be late. She had raised her hand to turn the latch of the front door, when she saw the letter. The door was fitted with one of those little wire baskets behind the letter-box, and she so seldom received correspondence of any sort that she had not troubled to look before. The postman must have rung the bell instead of knocking, and the bell had not been in working order for the past week.

She lifted the flap of the basket and took the letter out, and at that moment she heard a nearby clock begin to strike the hour. Thrusting the letter, unopened, into her pocket, she hurried down the stairs and almost ran along Grayling Street. It would take her ten minutes at the shortest to reach the office, and she was supposed to be there at nine o'clock. It was seldom that Mr. Hake was after that hour himself, but this morning was one of those rare occasions, and as she ran breathlessly up the stairs and entered the outer office the aged managing clerk shook his head with a smile — a sign that the head of the firm had not yet arrived, and which she greeted with relief. Hastily removing her hat and coat, she seated herself at her table, and then she remembered the letter that was in her pocket. She fetched it and looked with a puzzled frown at the envelope. It was a large and rather bulky letter, and it was addressed in typescript. She caught sight of the post-mark — Horsham — and was in the act of slitting open the flap when Mr. Hake's bell rang, and hurriedly putting the letter into her drawer, she went into the inner office.

'Good morning,' she said, and stood waiting.

The lawyer looked at her and through her. His usual healthy face was the colour of putty, and there were dark pouches under his eyes. He looked a very sick man indeed.

'Good morning, Miss Hardy,' he said absently, after a lengthy pause. 'Er — good morning — yes, let me see — ' He made a tremendous effort to collect his thoughts. 'Oh, yes, that agreement for Hill. Have you completed the draft?'

She nodded.

'Bring it here, will you?' he said, and she went and fetched it.

It was a long document, and for nearly an hour they went over it, while Mr. Hake suggested the alterations he would like. Suddenly in the midst of a clause he looked up.

'That woman's dead,' he said quite abruptly.

Betty stared at him.

'Woman — which woman?' she asked.

'Berman.' She was surprised to see that his hand was trembling violently. 'She was killed — murdered. It's in all the papers.'

Her eyes widened in horror. 'Murdered?' she stammered. 'When — why — I — '

'She was killed at her cottage at

Horsham the night before last. Nobody knows who did it or why.' He was staring not at her, but at a point immediately behind her, and almost involuntarily she looked round. There was nothing there.

'How — dreadful!' It seemed a feeble comment to make, but she could think of nothing else. A vision of the woman as she had last seen her, her face distorted with drink and temper, rose before her eyes.

'How was she killed?' she asked, and it was a long time before the solicitor answered, then he spoke so softly that his voice was the merest whisper of a whisper.

'Strangled.'

Betty shuddered. Whose hatred had the unpleasant Mrs. Berman aroused that it could only be assuaged by her death? And then, just as she had opened her lips to make a further remark, she remembered the post-mark on the letter she had received that morning.

Horsham!

Was it merely a coincidence, or was there something in that letter concerning the dead woman? She almost laughed at the absurdity of her imagination. Of course, there couldn't be! What should Mrs. Berman or any of her friends have to write to her about? Like a flash of brilliant light the idea came to her. Her father! There was something in that letter about her father —

'What's the matter with you? What are you looking like that for?' Mr. Hake's shrill and edgy voice snapped in on her thoughts.

'I — why — was I looking like anything?' she asked incoherently, and reddened.

'I don't know.' He snapped his fingers irritably. 'Don't take any notice of me. I'm not feeling very well this morning. I'll ring if I want you. Take that agreement away, and we'll look into it later. Don't stand there, girl, like a wooden doll! For God's sake go, and leave me alone!'

The last words shot out of his mouth as though something had snapped inside him. His mouth was twitching nervously, and Betty began to feel a little alarmed.

'Would you like me to get you

anything — ' she began, but he cut her off sharply.

'No,' he jerked, and without further delay she left the office. The communicating door was shut quickly behind her, and she heard the key turn in the lock.

But as she seated herself at her own table all thought of Mr. Hake passed completely from her mind. Her curiosity concerning the contents of the Horsham-marked letter was at fever heat. She took the envelope from her drawer and opened it. Inside was a letter and another envelope sealed and bearing a scrawled superscription:

'To be forwarded to Miss Betty Hardy, Flat 4, 29 Grayling Street, Bloomsbury, immediately after my death.'

'Bloomsbury' and 'immediately' were wrongly spelt.

She laid the sealed envelope beside her typewriter and read the letter with which it had been enclosed. It had a printed heading — 'Clifford & Shine, Solicitors,' and ran:

'Dear Madam,

On the twenty-first of October of last year we were given the enclosed by Mrs. Annie Berman, with instructions to forward it to you on her decease. These instructions we are now carrying out.

We should like it clearly understood that we are only obeying our late client's wishes in this matter, and have no knowledge whatsoever of the contents of the sealed envelope herewith enclosed. We feel, however, that having regard for the circumstances under which our client met her death, that it is our duty to inform the police that this envelope has been forwarded to you, in case it should contain anything that would be likely to assist them in their task of unravelling the mystery surrounding our late client's strange decease.

We are, madam,
Your obedient servants,
Clifford & Shine,
p.p. G.B.'

Betty read the letter twice, and then she

took up the sealed envelope and broke it open. Inside were three sheets of cheap writing paper covered with the same illiterate scrawl as the address. Spreading them out before her, the girl began to read.

And as she read her face whitened and her breath came faster, for here was the reason for Sir James Maddox's murder. Here, clearly set forth in Mrs. Berman's spidery writing with its bad spelling, was the story of a gigantic plot, and the names of those who were concerned in it. So absorbed was she that she failed to hear the buzzer go above her table, or the key turn in the lock and the communicating door leading to Mr. Hake's office open.

'What's that you're reading? What's that, girl?' The solicitor's voice, hoarse, almost a croak, caused her to look up with a start. He was standing behind her and staring over her shoulder with bulging eyes at Mrs. Berman's statement. Before she could move or reply he had snatched it from her hand.

'My God!' he breathed as he caught sight of a few lines, and his face showed the terror that had gripped his soul.

'Give that to me, please, Mr. Hake,' said Betty steadily, though his expression frightened her.

He said nothing, but he crushed the thin sheets into his pocket and came towards her.

'You've read this — you know!' he said between his teeth, and she opened her lips to scream. He caught her by the throat, and his huge hand covered her mouth and choked back the cry.

She struggled hard to free herself, and her teeth met in the fleshy palm. But Hake was beyond feeling pain. Still holding her tightly, he glanced round him, and presently his eyes found what they sought — a heavy ebony ruler that lay beside her typewriter. Releasing his hold of her throat, but still keeping one hand over her mouth, he picked it up and brought it down with all his force on her head. A rush of darkness blotted out his distorted face, the office, everything, and she collapsed limply into his arms!

24

The Sentence!

Panting from his exertion, Mr. Hake let her slip gently to the floor and going over to the door giving access to the outer office, locked it quickly. What he had done, he had done on the spur of the moment. There had been no other way, but the risk was enormous! At any moment his managing clerk or a client might seek admittance and — he shivered. For perhaps thirty seconds he stood motionless, and then he acted swiftly. With his handkerchief and some stout cord he gagged and bound the girl securely and picking her up, carried her into his own private office. There was a large cupboard built into the wall in one corner, and opening this, Mr. Hake shifted the stacks of papers and books to one side until there was room for the unconscious girl. He put her in and then went back for her hat and coat and laid them on the top of her. Closing and locking the cupboard door, he wiped his perspiring face with a fresh handkerchief that he found in his overcoat. As soon as he had regained his normal appearance, he went into the outer office.

The aged clerk looked up from his work.

'Oh — er — Wenner,' said Mr. Hake pleasantly, 'will you attend to Miss Hardy's work for the rest of the day? She wasn't feeling at all well and I've sent her home.'

This was quite a plausible excuse for the disappearance of the girl, for there was a way out from the lawyer's private office that opened directly into the corridor and one could leave without passing through either Betty's or the outer office.

'Yes, sir,' answered Wenner. 'I'm sorry to hear about Miss Hardy, sir. Shall I move into her office?'

'Yes.' The solicitor nodded. 'I think that would be the best plan.'

Wenner rose and began collecting up

his papers and Hake went back into his own office and sat down behind his desk. So far so good, but the girl couldn't be kept in the cupboard indefinitely. Something would have to be done. He waited until he heard Wenner settle down in the girl's room and then he drew the telephone towards him and gave a number. For some time he held a conversation with the person at the other end, and when at last he hung up the receiver he looked more cheerful. His difficulty had been disposed of and so, incidentally, had Betty Hardy.

For the rest of the day he transacted his ordinary business, though his mind was not wholly on his work, and at his usual time he left the office and went home.

At half past ten that night a constable patrolling slowly along Bedford Row saw a closed car standing by the kerb and would have passed on with only a casual glance, if at that moment he had not noticed two men come out of a doorway carrying a large trunk. He stopped. The house was not a private residence but was given over to offices, and he was rather

302

suspicious. He was in the act of accosting the men when he recognised that one of them was the tenant of a suite.

'Oh, it's you, Mr. Hake,' he said touching his helmet. 'I thought perhaps it might be burglars.'

The solicitor laughed, and if it was a trifle forced the policeman noticed nothing.

'I'm burgling my own office, officer,' he said lightly. 'Taking away a lot of old agreements and leases.'

'I thought it was red tape, sir,' said the policeman with a chuckle, and he waited while the trunk was strapped securely on the back of the car. The man who was helping Hake, and whose face the constable had not seen, got into the driving seat and the solicitor climbed in beside him, and as the car glided away from the kerb, the watching policeman was quite unaware that he had missed the greatest chance of promotion that had ever come his way!

But he was not the only man who had witnessed that visit paid so late at night by the solicitor to his office. A man who had been tinkering with a motorcycle a hundred yards up the street, suddenly seemed to have put whatever had been wrong with his machine right, for he straightened up, slipped astride the saddle and went chugging off in the wake of the disappearing car.

It was his job to follow Mr. Hake wherever he might go and he was carrying it out conscientiously.

* * *

Betty came slowly to her senses and the return to consciousness was not pleasant. Her mouth and throat were dry and parched and her eyes burned. There was a dull throbbing pain in her head that was like the beating of huge hammers on her brain, and she felt physically sick. She wondered vaguely what had happened and presently as she got more and more alert, little jumbled fragments came back to her. The letter . . . Hake . . . and she remembered!

She tried to move, but found that it was impossible and discovered that her wrists and ankles were securely tied, and that a gag had been fastened in her mouth. She wondered where she was, but it was difficult to answer this question for she was in pitch darkness, and beyond the fact that she was lying on something soft in a place that smelt damp and musty, she could give no guess as to her whereabouts.

She was not at the office in Bedford Row — of that she was certain. What, then, had Hake done with her?

There was no reason to ask why she had been treated like this. Only too vividly she remembered the contents of that letter and realised that she held in her possession knowledge that was sufficient to send the solicitor to prison for a long sentence and bring two other people to the gallows.

After lying for some considerable time in that pitch blackness she began to feel better. The pain in her head subsided and the nausea went away. She would have given almost anything for a cup of tea, and began to realise that she was getting hungry. She had no idea of the time, but she concluded that several hours must have passed since the solicitor had attacked her in the office.

She had recovered from the blow he had given her to find herself in the cupboard and it had been much later that he had come and given her the drug that had robbed her for the second time of her senses.

Betty was a very ordinary, sensible girl, without the slightest touch of the modern complaint of hysteria in her constitution, and she wondered quite calmly what they would do with her. She rather wondered herself at her calmness, for she knew the sort of people she was dealing with and had no illusion regarding them.

They had killed three times already in order to preserve their secret, and certainly wouldn't hesitate a fourth time, if it suited them. And there was no reason why they should wish to keep her alive. On the contrary, her death would be an advantage to them. There seemed little hope then, unless her disappearance was discovered and somebody found her. She thought of Peter, but the probability of the reporter, or of anyone else, for that matter, coming to her rescue in time, was remote. If they were going to kill her they would do so at once — long before anyone realised that anything had happened to her.

A sound broke in on her thoughts and she saw somewhere in the darkness a slit of light appear. There was a grating sound and the ribbon of light widened as the door was opened and she made out the dim figure of a man carrying an oil lamp. He set it down on the floor and closed and re-locked the door. Then he came towards her. He was wearing an overcoat and hat and his face was hidden behind a handkerchief that had been bound loosely round his nose and chin.

He looked down at her for some seconds and then he took a pistol from his pocket and bent forward. For the first time Betty felt a shiver of fear. Had he come to kill her already? But he only loosened the gag and pulled it away from her mouth.

'It's no good your attempting to shout or scream,' he said gruffly. 'No one will hear you and if you try anything like that I shall kill you now. Here, I've brought you some food.'

He took a packet from the pocket of his overcoat and produced from it a thermos flask and some sandwiches. Propping the girl up against the wall, he held the flask to her lips and she drank the coffee it contained greedily.

'Now eat some of these.' He fed her with the sandwiches, holding them so as to avoid the necessity of undoing the cords at her wrists.

While she ate she took stock of her surroundings in the dim light of the lantern and saw that the place to which she had been brought was a small cellar. The walls and floor were of stone and so was the roof — thick, heavy slabs of rough hewn stone. The dust on the floor was inches thick — she could see the lines of foot-prints that ran towards the door — and the place was devoid of anything in the nature of furniture, with the exception of the low couch on which she was sitting, and which she had noticed was modern and new. The man watched her eyes as she looked about and noted the expression on her face.

'Not much of a place, is it?' he asked. 'Oh well, you won't be here long, so it doesn't matter.'

'What's going to happen to me?' she asked, and he shrugged his shoulders and brushed the crumbs off his coat.

'You're going to die!' he said without emotion of any kind. 'I don't know whether it will be to-night or to-morrow or the day after, but you're going to die before the week's out!'

Before she could reply he had pulled up the gag and refastened it, and then without another word he picked up the lamp, unlocked the door and went out. It closed with a clang and the key turned, leaving her alone with the darkness and her thoughts.

25

The Man who Knew

REPORTER MURDERED!
BODY FOUND SHOT DEAD IN WOOD!

The newsboys shouted it. The flaring placards displayed it in heavy block type, and the public rushed to buy the papers eagerly, pushing their pennies into the moist hands of the newsvendors, and snatching the papers still wet from the press. It was the sole topic of conversation in tube, and train and bus, in the East End and in the West End, in London and in the provinces, for it was connected with the Maddox murder, and that case had taken hold of the public's imagination.

Chief-Inspector Trimmer of Scotland Yard read the report gloomily and said nothing. Dick Mason heard the account of the murder from his gaoler, and was in despair. The man who might have saved him was not in a position to save anybody. Mr. Hake, of Hake, Rand & Hake smiled to himself, and read the news again with infinite pleasure, and Mr. Frank Rabson, seated in his sitting-room in the house in Rose Water Lane, Battersea, drank a silent toast in neat whisky to the man who had been responsible for the reporter's death.

Peter's body, according to the newspapers, had been found in the wood near the point at which his car had been abandoned. There was a thicket of close-growing briars, in the midst of which was a deep depression that had probably at one time been a ditch, and it was in this that the search party had discovered the remains. So thickly did the undergrowth and bushes grow over the place that it was overlooked in the first search. The reporter had been shot through the head and, also according to the newspaper account, the police had no clue to the identity of his murderer.

The man who knew all about it and

had been responsible for all the excitement naturally said nothing, but he read the varying accounts, and wondered silently what would happen if he walked into the offices of any one of these newspapers, and told his story. He was under no illusion as to the sensation it would cause. He was not a very prepossessing individual as he sat before the fire in his little cottage eating his supper of bread and cheese and pickles. His face was dirty and partly concealed by a beard and moustache that had seen a pair of scissors perhaps half a dozen times in his life. His hair was thick and flecked with grey and grew low on his forehead, almost meeting the bushy eyebrows that overhung his deep-set eyes.

The room in which he sat was like the man, untidy and dirty. The floor had not been brushed or scrubbed for months, and the plain deal table in the centre was littered with the dirty dishes of innumerable meals. But it was a palace in comparison to Daniel Hocket's last abode, for they are not given to making the cells at Portland luxurious though they are certainly clean, and Mr. Hocket had spent more than half his life at that celebrated prison. He drained a large jug of beer, drinking it with noisy relish, and then lighting a short clay pipe, he lay back in the only armchair the place boasted, and stared into the wood fire. Once more before his eyes he conjured up that scene on the darkened stretch of road, the darkness made darker by comparison with the headlights of the car. He had done a good night's work that night if he had ever done one. After disposing of his victim he had been unusually busy long after the dawn broke, and when he finally reached this cottage, he was dog tired but conscious of having accomplished something worthwhile.

The garden at Maddox Court had not seen him all the next day. He had sent a message up to the house to say that he was ill. For Mr. Hocket was the gardener to that pretentious establishment, and had secured the job through the good auspices of his friend, Mr. Hake. The lawyer had supplied him with the necessary references, and it is needless to remark that they made no mention of his sojourn in Portland or in any other prison. Nor when he engaged him was Sir James aware of the real character of the man he had taken into his employ. There was a certain file, however, at Scotland Yard that set out Mr. Hocket's hobbies and recreations with unqualified truth, and a certain amount of harshness. There were six convictions for robbery with violence, mostly attacks on women in deserted country roads or lonely commons. By the aid of a length of lead piping Mr. Hocket had managed in this manner to acquire an uncertain livelihood, and earn for himself the nickname of 'Basher.' As Basher Hocket he was known to the police, and to those penal establishments that he had graced with his presence. Across his shoulders were several long scars, the mark that the cat had left for his last offence, a particularly unpleasant and brutal affair, but all this was past history.

For six months Mr. Hocket had been an honest man, earning his bread by the sweat of his brow. At least he presented that illusion, though he left most of the actual sweating to the two youths who worked under him, and were really responsible for the well-kept appearance of the garden at Maddox Court. Basher Hocket had a deep-rooted antipathy to work, and although he did not object to a little pruning, and occasional planting of bulbs and such-like light duties, the mere thought of a lawn mower made him feel physically ill. He had been placed in the position of gardener by Mr. Hake, but it was not because of any anxiety on that gentleman's part concerning the welfare of Sir James Maddox's flowers. His presence was for quite another reason, but a certain appearance had to be kept up for the sake of the other members of the household.

Sitting gazing at the dying fire, and puffing at the coarse tobacco in his pipe, he pondered over the next move. He was not afraid that anyone would discover the part he had played in that incident of the lonely road. He had covered his tracks too well, and it was by a very circuitous route indeed that he had reached the cottage.

No, he did not think there was any risk of discovery, but since he was playing such a big part in the business, he would have liked to know what lay behind it. He knew that Hake was hatching some gigantic plot, but he didn't know its details. He was to a large extent in the dark, although he was beginning to have a pretty good idea. The time went by and still he sat there thinking, until the pipe was cold between his lips. Presently he tapped the ashes out on the heel of his boot, and was reloading the bowl from a battered pouch, when a noise outside made him suddenly alert. It was the faint sound of a footfall. It drew nearer, paused, and then there came a soft tapping on the door. The bearded man rose clumsily to his feet, crossed over and drew back the bolt. Framed against the dark sky was the figure of a man.

'Come out!' said the newcomer in a low voice. 'I want a word with you.'

'Why not 'ave it inside?' grunted the other, jerking his head towards the interior of the cottage.

'Don't be a fool!' was the retort. 'We

might be seen. Come into the woods; it's darker and safer there.'

The bearded man shrugged his shoulders and stepped across the threshold, closing the door behind him. The cottage was situated on the fringe of a wood, and was in reality nothing more than a charcoal burner's hut, for it possessed but one floor, and this had been divided into two small rooms. The man called Hocket followed his companion into the shadow of the trees, and under a large oak he stopped.

'Now,' he said, 'tell me all about it. You managed the job all right?'

'Looks like it, don't it?' growled the gardener. 'Oh, yes, I managed it all right, you betcher life. The third shot went clean through 'is 'ead, clean as a whistle.' He chuckled at the recollection.

'And you're sure you left no trace?' said the other anxiously. 'Nothing that might lead the police to suspect you?'

Hocket shook his head. 'Nothin',' he answered. 'I took partic'lar care.'

'How was it you had to fire three times?' asked the man sharply.

''cos I trod on a ruddy dead branch!'
retorted Hocket, 'and 'e 'eard me just
before I let fly with the first bullet. 'e
dodged that and the second too, but the
third finished 'im.'

'You've done very well,' said the other,
'and you'll be well paid.'

'I should 'ope so!' muttered Hocket.
'I've put me neck in danger and that
ought to be worth a bit.'

'I said you'll be well paid,' snapped the
other, 'another month at the outside
should see the whole of this business
cleared up. I thought that damned
reporter was going to be troublesome at
first, but now he's out of the way
everything is plain sailing.'

'I wish you'd let me in on the graft,'
grumbled the gardener. 'It ain't easy
workin' in the dark, and 'ake's as close as
an oyster. 'e won't let on.'

'He's quite right,' snarled the tall
man. 'It's not your business. All you've
got to do is to do as you're told, and
take your money for doing it. And if
you're feeling curious just check it at
once; we don't like curious people. Mrs.

Berman was curious, and you know what happened to her.'

'All right, all right,' Hocket said hastily. 'I ain't grumblin'. You've promised to pay me well, an' I ain't fool enough to risk losin' that.'

'You're a wise man.' There was the hint of a sneer in the deep voice. 'Continue to be wise. Now I must go. There's one other job for you to do to-morrow night, and you can make it as late as you like. It would be awkward if you were seen.'

'What's that?' asked the gardener without enthusiasm. 'What ye want done now?'

His companion leaned forward and whispered in his ear, and Hocket looked startled.

'In the wood?' he said hoarsely.

The other nodded. 'In the thickest part of the wood,' he replied, 'and make it deep.'

'Who's it for?' asked the bearded man.

'You'll know when the time comes,' was the retort. 'Remember what I said about curiosity.'

He uttered a curt good night and

strode away, vanishing in the darkness.

The bearded man stood for some time at the place where his companion had left him, deep in thought. Then, turning, he went back to the cottage, bolted the door, and kicking the fire into a blaze, dropped into the armchair. His forehead was furrowed and his eyes were narrowed, for his brain was busy, and the question that puzzled him was this: he had been instructed to dig a grave and he was wondering who the occupant was to be.

26

The Grave in the Wood

Betty had no idea of the passing of time. It seemed to her that she had been confined in that dark and musty cellar-like room for ages. At intervals food was brought to her by her gaoler and in between whiles she slept fitfully, an unrestful sleep that was troubled by hideous dreams from which she woke with a scream in her throat and bathed in cold perspiration.

She wondered why she was still alive. The people who held her had everything to gain by her death. It was essential to their safety that she should never be able to speak of the contents of the letter that Mrs. Berman had sent her. Why, then, did they delay the inevitable by keeping her alive? Had her death been planned and was the time not yet ripe? That was the only explanation.

She felt years older than she had done when Hake had struck her down in the little office in Bedford Row. The suspense and the constant fear had played havoc with her nerves, and she wondered once — and smiled wanly at the conceit — what she looked like. With the knowledge of impending death hanging over her, life had never seemed sweeter or more desirable. While she lay in that dense blackness, unrelieved by a chink of light, she recalled many incidents of her life — stupid, forgotten little happenings that in normal circumstances would never have crossed her mind, but now became magnified to a degree utterly beyond their worth.

Little pictures of her annual holiday — saved for and looked forward to — crowded through her brain. Her first meeting with Dick at the small tea shop where they had both been in the habit of going for lunch and the prosaic sugar-basin which had been the means of introduction. She had a sudden longing for a glimpse of the sun and the sky and to smell the fresh air after a fall of rain

— for the smell that is London and the shops and the crowded streets, her cosy little flat and the quiet squares through which she had so often walked to her work. It was wonderful what real pleasure lay in the ordinary daily routine of life — pleasures she had scarcely considered until now, when there seemed a prospect of losing them for ever. She wondered why everybody who had health and was free could not be happy, and remembered the many times she had been depressed and miserable for no very particular reason at all — just because she hadn't enough money for a new hat or a frock or a pair of shoes. How stupid it all seemed now!

The tears welled up to her eyes and ran slowly down her cheeks until she could taste the salt of them beneath the gag. She turned over on her side to ease her cramped limbs and wondered whether it was light or dark outside this prison — day or night. So far as she could judge by a vague guess, she had been in this place now for three days. It seemed longer and it might be less, but that was as near as she could tell — and then she heard the familiar approaching footsteps of her gaoler. The door swung slowly open and she shrank back against the wall — as she always did on these occasions, for she never knew when this would prove to be the visit she dreaded — that final visit that would spell the end of all things.

He came over and stood looking down at her, the lamp swinging in his hand. 'I've come to take you away,' he said after a pause and, setting down the light, took a long knife from his pocket.

But for the gag she would have screamed and he must have seen the terror in her eyes, for he laughed.

'You needn't be afraid of this — yet,' he said. 'I am only going to use it as a means of precaution.'

He stooped and cut the cords that bound her ankles.

'Get up,' he ordered harshly, and she swung her legs off the settee. But she couldn't stand. Her limbs were numb from the long-checked circulation and he had to rub her ankles for nearly five minutes before she recovered the use of them. Even then the pain was so great that she bit into her gag in her agony. Presently, however, it subsided and she was able to get weakly to her feet.

'Come with me,' he said, and taking her arm led her towards the door. 'And remember that I've got this knife and don't try any tricks.'

They passed through the heavy door, which she noticed was made of oak, and into a narrow brick passage beyond. The walls were coated with the dirt and grime of centuries and the roof was so low that they had to stoop. The passage twisted and turned from right to left and from left to right, and then ended in a flight of steps that led upward.

The man behind pushed her up the steps until they stopped at a long, narrow door. Her captor blew out the lamp and then, in the darkness, she heard a faint click and felt a rush of air blowing on her face. She was pushed through into total darkness but guessed that she was in some kind of a room. There was a faint smell of flowers and then her arm was gripped and she was dragged forward once again.

Her feet sank into thick carpet and then onto bare boards and she was directed down a narrow flight of uncarpeted stairs. There was a rattle of chains and bolts and a door swung open. The refreshing sting of rain lashed her face and she found herself in the open air. She caught sight of the shadowy trunks of trees towering above her and heard the moan of the wind in their branches.

'This way,' whispered the man who held her arm and led her along a winding path between clumps of straggling bushes and then, as he halted, she saw the dim outline of a car without lights before her.

Without releasing his hold he pulled open a door and thrust her into the machine, getting in beside her and taking his place behind the wheel. She heard the whining purr of the self-starter and then the deeper throb of the engine and the car began to move.

It swung round and gathered speed and they shot off into the night. Where was she being taken, and what lay at the end of the journey? She tried to see where they were but the rain blurred the windows of the closed coupé and all she could make out was an indistinct ribbon of passing hedges on either side.

The ride was not a long one. They had barely been travelling for a quarter of an hour before her captor stopped the machine and signed to her to get out. She stepped on to a soggy, rutted road and looked about her. Near at hand was a thick wood — they had stopped on the fringe of it — and half-concealed by the trees she saw a faint light. It came from the window of a hut-like building and towards this the man led her.

Pausing at the door, he tapped gently, and after a lapse of time she heard a movement within, and a bearded man appeared on the threshold.

'Have you finished it?' asked the man who held her abruptly, and the bearded man nodded.

'Yes,' he answered, 'half an hour ago.'

She saw that his sleeves were rolled up and his hands and arms were stained with mud up to the elbows.

'Good,' replied the other with satisfaction. 'Then I'll leave the rest of the business to you. Be careful when you fill it in afterwards — that you leave the ground looking as undisturbed as possible.'

'It wouldn't matter whether I did or not,' answered the bearded man. 'Nobody ever goes near the place where I've dug it.' He looked at Betty. 'Is this — who it's for?'

'Yes,' said her captor shortly.

Hocket frowned. 'Why did yer say yer'd leave the rest to me?' he demanded. 'Yer don't expect me ter — ter — '

'I expect you to do as you're told,' broke in the other harshly. 'What's the good of keeping a dog and barking yourself?'

Hocket shook his head. 'I ain't going to do any more of that,' he protested. 'I did my last job at that sort of thing when I finished off that feller. You do your own dirty work!'

'You'll do what you're told,' hissed the man, his face convulsed with rage. 'I'm not standing any nonsense from you, Hocket. You're getting well paid and

328

you've got to earn it.' He leaned forward and said something in a low voice that Betty could not hear. It had its effect on the bearded man. The truculence in his voice faded.

'Awl right,' he muttered. 'I'll do what yer want.'

'I thought you'd be sensible,' was the cool reply. 'Now, I'm going.' He pulled the terrified girl forward and the bearded man gripped her arm.

'You'll need this,' said the other, thrusting the knife into his hand. 'Don't forget that your own neck as well as mine depends on your making a good job of it, so don't bungle.' He turned away and Betty heard the car engine throb to life.

'Come on,' growled the bearded man as she tried to struggle free. 'It's no good making a fuss.'

He dragged her half-fainting with fear towards the wood and as they reached the shadow of the trees she heard the purr of the car fade in the distance.

'Now,' said Hocket, and he raised the knife!

27

Frank Lane Behaves Strangely

The solicitors who had forwarded Mrs. Berman's letter to Betty Hardy in accordance with the dead woman's wishes kept their promise and notified the Horsham police. The Horsham police got in touch with London, and requested that somebody should be sent to Grayling Street to see Betty and find out what the letter contained. A certain Sergeant Buffton was dispatched from Scotland Yard on this errand, and duly arrived at the girl's tiny flat. But nobody answered his repeated knocking, and an enquiry to the next door neighbour resulted in the statement that 'she didn't think Miss Hardy had been home for some days.' Checked at this point, the detective-sergeant discovered that the girl was employed at Messrs. Hake, Rand & Hake and went off to Bedford Row to interview the solicitor. Mr. Hake greeted him gravely, and evinced the greatest surprise when he heard that his secretary was not at her flat.

'Extraordinary!' he exclaimed. 'No, I don't attempt to explain it unless she's gone away for a few days. She complained of not feeling well the other morning, and I told her to go home and come back when she was better. As she didn't come back I concluded that she was still indisposed. In fact, to be quite candid with you, I was going round this afternoon to see what had happened to her.' He had had no such intention, but he thought it sounded better to say so.

'Had she any friends she may have gone to — and relations, sir?' asked the sergeant.

The lawyer shook his large head. 'Not that I know about,' he answered. 'No, I don't know where she can have gone to. It's extraordinary.' He held out a case of cigars to the sergeant, and that worthy man took one and lit it with extreme care.

'Can you' — Mr. Hake hesitated as though aware that he was asking a great favour — 'can you inform me why you are making these enquiries?'

Sergeant Buffton not only could, but did, and the lawyer drew heavy brows together in a puzzled frown.

'Good gracious me, that's amazing!' he said in astonishment. 'Amazing! What could poor Mrs. Berman have had to write to Miss Hardy about, and why did she entrust her letter to another firm of solicitors when we have always acted for her? She knew me so well.'

Sergeant Buffton thought that possibly this might have been the reason, but he kept his thoughts to himself.

'I can't understand it at all,' declared Mr. Hake when the officer was taking his departure. 'It's a complete mystery to me. I trust that you will let me know directly you discover what has happened to the girl.'

The sergeant did not promise anything of the sort, but he made some vague reply and went back to the Yard. He reported his failure to locate the girl to Chief-Inspector Trimmer, and that melancholy man ran a lean hand through his grizzled hair.

'I don't like it,' he muttered. 'I don't like it at all! Where can the girl have got to? Go and take a man and have a look round her flat. Don't break in. Pick the lock, and then report again.'

Sergeant Buffton turned away, and as he was going out of the door Mr. Trimmer added: 'You might ask them to send that fellow up from Cannon Row.'

He sat for some time staring across his desk at the opposite wall, and his expression was very thoughtful. The cyclist detective, who had been put on to watch Mr. Hake had lost him in a traffic block, so where the lawyer had gone on the night that he had left Bedford Row, nobody knew.

Presently the 'fellow from Cannon Row' was brought in under the guard of two detectives, and a more unpleasant-looking specimen it would have been difficult to find. He stood sullenly before the chief-inspector, answering the latter's string of questions with monosyllabic replies, and after nearly an hour had gone by, Mr. Trimmer jerked his head at the detectives. 'Take him back to the 'cooler,'' he snapped, and the man was led away.

Later on that evening there was a conference at Scotland Yard. It was attended by Major Hilling and Inspector Burnett, and the superintendent of the Horsham police, and was presided over by Chief-Inspector Trimmer. For nearly three hours they talked and argued, and consulted various bulky folders and reports, and while they talked in London, Mr. Frank Lane sat sipping his coffee in the long dining-room at Maddox Court, and talked to his cousin.

Margaret Maddox was looking more than usually attractive in the simple black frock she was wearing, and at that precise moment was shaking her honey-coloured head at a remark that Mr. Lane had just made.

'I don't know why you should dislike him, Frank,' she said. 'He's been terribly kind since poor Daddy's death.' Her voice broke slightly.

'I'm not saying he hasn't,' argued Mr. Lane, sniffing through his long thin nose. 'After all, it pays him to be attentive to you. If he succeeds in making himself sufficiently indispensable, he may not lose his job.'

'That's a particularly nasty thing to say!' she said, flushing.

'I mean it, anyhow,' answered the other. 'You can stick up for Stroude as much as you like, but I can't stand the fellow.'

'Why?' she asked. 'What's your objection to him?'

'I can't go anywhere without him,' he grumbled. 'He follows me about like a shadow. If I go into the garden I find Stroude. If I go into the drawing-room he comes in a few seconds after. I can't go anywhere without that confounded fellow at my heels.'

'What nonsense!' exclaimed Margaret. 'It must be just a coincidence. Why should he follow you about?'

'Goodness only knows, but he does,' said Mr. Lane. He lighted a cigarette and held his case out to the girl.

'I'm sure it's only your imagination.' She tapped the cigarette she had taken on the polished wood in front of her. 'You never did like him — even when Father was alive.'

'And I never shall! I'm not at all sure that Stroude doesn't know more about the death of the old man than he has said.' He growled out the words irritably, and the girl uttered a low cry.

'How can you say such things!' she exclaimed.

'I mean it!' declared Mr. Lane, pouring himself out another glass of port. 'There's more in this murder than appears on the surface.'

'I think it's beastly of you to accuse a man without the slightest proof,' she said indignantly.

He flicked the ash from his cigarette impatiently into his plate. 'I'm not accusing him of the crime,' he retorted. 'I'm not accusing anybody. But you must admit that the whole business is fishy. Why should Uncle have been killed at all, what motive was there?'

'I don't know,' she replied under her breath, 'but Mr. Stroude couldn't possibly have had one. Daddy's death robs him of a very comfortable situation.'

Mr. Lane drew his reddish brows into a frown. 'That seems to be true,' he admitted. 'But somebody did it and I'm inclined to doubt the original idea that it was that fellow whom Stroude found bending over the body.'

'Don't, please!' she broke in quickly, her face even paler than usual. 'It's all so — so fresh in my memory, and you know how fond I was of Daddy . . . '

'I'm sorry, Margaret,' he apologised, but there was no touch of sorrow in his voice. 'I was fond of the old man, too, and I'm only trying to get to the bottom of the mystery. As I was saying, that fellow Mason doesn't appear to have had anything to do with it after all. He was locked up at the time Annie was killed. Neither could he have had anything to do with the shooting of that unfortunate reporter.' He crushed out the stub of his cigarette. 'I wonder why Annie Berman was murdered? It must be all part of the same business, but I'm hanged if I can see the reason.'

He was going on to say more but at that moment the door opened and Charles Stroude came in.

'I have written to Hake asking him to

make an appointment for to-morrow, Miss Maddox,' he said in a business-like manner. 'I suggested some time in the afternoon. Will that be convenient for you?'

She nodded and the secretary turned to Mr. Lane. 'I've no doubt you'd like to be present, sir, when we go through Sir James's documents,' he said. 'I mentioned in my letter that you were staying here for a few days.'

'I should most certainly like to be present,' remarked Frank Lane.

'I have asked Mr. Hake to telephone as early as possible, and say what time he is arriving,' said Stroude. 'I'll let you know as soon as I hear from him.'

He lingered a moment or two and then left them, and as soon as he had gone Margaret rose and excused herself on the plea that she had some letters to write.

Mr. Frank Lane remained seated at the table for some time, smoking and gazing thoughtfully before him, and it was not until the maids came to clear away the dinner things that he moved. The rest of the evening he spent in the drawing-room, reading. Though from the fact that by the time he retired to bed the book still remained open at the same page, it would appear doubtful if he knew much about the story.

It was getting on for eleven when he went to his bedroom, and almost the first thing he saw when he switched on the light was a letter lying on his pillow by the side of his pyjama case. He picked it up, glanced at the superscription with a frown, and tore open the flap. Twice he read the closely written sheet it contained, and then going over to the fireplace, he took a box of matches from his pocket and carefully burned the letter, crushing the tinder to dust in the grate. And he did not go to bed. Seated in a chair, he waited while the house gradually settled down to sleep. He heard Gilder go his rounds, fastening the windows, and locking and bolting the doors; heard the old clock in the hall strike twelve, one, and the half hour. And then he went to the door and listened. There was no sound from the sleeping house, and going back into his bedroom, Mr. Lane took a heavy coat from his wardrobe and put it on. Wrapping a scarf round his throat, he pulled a cap down over his eyes, and began to creep softly along the corridor to the head of the staircase. Moving without making a sound on the thick carpet, he cautiously descended the stairs. Once near the bottom a tread creaked loudly. In the stillness it sounded almost like a pistol shot, and he paused, his heart in his mouth. Apparently it had not disturbed anyone, however, and presently he continued on his way. Crossing the hall he felt along the wall, until he reached the door that led to the kitchen. It was unlocked, and pushing it open he negotiated the narrow staircase beyond. At the end of a short passage was the back door that opened into the garden. He had some difficulty in removing the chain, and pulling back the bolts, but he succeeded without making more than a slight amount of noise, and opened the door gently. The darkness of the night was intense, and he peered out, shivering as a cold gust of wind came whining round the corner of the house. Closing the door, he stepped out on to the gravel of the path, and as he did so a man who had been standing in the shelter of a clump of shrubbery moved forward and touched him on the arm.

'Is that you?' whispered a voice.

'Yes,' said Mr. Lane.

'Come along, then. We can't talk here; somebody might hear us,' said the other, and walking side by side the two disappeared into the shadows of the night.

28

The Midnight Meeting

Smoke was coming from the little hut belonging to Daniel Hocket. A small fire burned in the choked grate, and the inhabitant of the cottage, with a fork in his hand, was watching the sizzling chop that spluttered in the frying pan he held over the glowing wood. The cheap tin clock on the mantelpiece pointed to a few minutes to one, and this was his first meal of that day. He had been exceedingly busy from daybreak to nightfall. Behind the cottage in the dark and unpleasant little wood, the grave had been completely filled in, the surface of the ground flattened down and covered with brambles and bushes. Only he knew what lay beneath that disturbed soil. He had worked nearly all through the night after he had disposed of the girl, and then snatching a few hours' sleep had gone on again during the ensuing day, though it was different work he did then.

The man who had brought Betty Hardy to the cottage and left her in the tender care of its occupant would not have been best pleased had he known what Hocket was engaged in doing. For after much thought he had come to the conclusion that he wanted to know a lot more about his employer. He knew the name but that was not enough; neither was the reward he had been offered for his services sufficient to prevent his being curious. There was a bigger reward to be had, if only he could find out what was at the bottom of this business, and with infinite care he had set to work and found out. And now, later that night, after he had had his meal, he intended to put into execution another part of his scheme.

The letter he had written earlier to Mr. Frank Lane had been placed on that gentleman's pillow. He had managed to slip it there while the rest of the household were at dinner, and he knew that Mr. Lane would obey the summons. Presently he would go up to the house and wait for him, and bring him down to the cottage and they would have a heart-to-heart talk. He wondered as he speared the chop from the pan and dropped it onto the hot plate before the fire, what Mr. Lane would say when he knew that he had discovered the whole plot. The bearded man shrugged his shoulders. It was of very little interest to him what Lane said. He would have to do as he was told.

He felt a certain amount of elation as he fetched bread and beer from a cupboard, and sat down to his frugal meal. Pushing the dirty plate away when he had finished, he filled and lit his short clay pipe, and then began to make preparations for his expedition. Putting on his hat, he unlatched the door, wedging it with a piece of wood so that it would not blow to during his absence, and then set off across the intervening ground that separated the hut from Maddox Court. He reached the back door just before half-past one, and had to wait nearly twenty minutes before he saw it cautiously opened and Mr. Lane appear.

He moved forward and grasped the other by the arm. 'We'll go to my cottage,' he breathed after the first preliminary remarks had been exchanged. 'We're not likely to be disturbed there.'

'Why have you chosen this hour?' asked Mr. Lane. 'Why drag me out at this time of night?'

'Because it's necessary,' was the short reply. 'Don't talk; we might be heard.' The other grunted something but relapsed into silence.

And so without further word they reached the hut in the wood.

'Sit down,' said the bearded man, barring the door. 'Now you know why I've brought you here, and what you don't know I'm going to tell you.'

He proceeded to do so, and Mr. Lane's sallow face grew longer and longer as he went on.

'Good God!' he exclaimed when the other finally finished. 'You know all that?'

'I know all that,' said the gardener.

'Well, what do you want?' asked Mr. Lane.

Daniel Hocket told him.

In the darkness of a rainy evening — much the same kind of evening as that on which Mr. William Sneath had left his little attic room, and gone forth full of optimism on what had eventually led to his death — a long police car swung into the narrow purlieus of Rose Water Lane, Battersea and drew up outside the house of Mr. Frank Rabson. Mr. Rabson was in, but by the time Detective-Sergeant Buffton had finished what he had to say he wished that he had been out. As a matter of fact, he was out fairly quickly, for he was escorted to the waiting car, and with handcuffs on his wrists was whisked away to Cannon Row, that convenient police station that is but an extension of Scotland Yard. In the discomfort of a cold cell he was left to meditate on the hardness of his past, and to conjecture vaguely what was likely to be his future, an occupation that seemed to afford him little amusement if the expression of his face was anything to go by.

Chief-Inspector Trimmer came in to see him after a long interval, and at first

Rabson tried to bluster. A few words from the lean man, however, and he collapsed like a pricked balloon.

'All right, I'll make a statement,' he growled.

'You're makin' it of your own free will, you know,' warned the chief-inspector. 'You haven't been forced to it in any way. I've merely told you what I know, that's all.'

'I know the law,' snarled Mr. Rabson. 'You couldn't make me say anythin' if I didn't want to.'

'That's not the only part of the case you'll know before you're much older,' retorted Mr. Trimmer, and he sent for a shorthand typist.

Mr. Frank Rabson's statement was a long one. At the end of two hours they were still busily taking it down.

'Do you want to make any alterations?' asked Mr. Trimmer as the man read it over, and Mr. Rabson shook his head. 'Then sign it and let's get finished,' said the chief-inspector wearily.

He was tired and not without reason,

for he had had no sleep for twenty-four hours.

Mr. Rabson took the pen that was held out to him, and with the signing of his name sent two people to the gallows.

*   *   *

Mr. Hake closed the door of his office in Bedford Row, tried it carefully to see that it was fastened properly, and began slowly to descend the stairs. He had reached the street when a thick-set man who had been waiting outside for the past half hour touched him on the arm. Mr. Hake swung round.

'What do you want?' he asked, and his voice was not quite steady.

'I want you!' answered the man from Scotland Yard. 'I'm Detective Inspector Marker of the Criminal Investigation Department. I shouldn't advise you to resist. There's a constable within call.'

'What — what do you mean — resist?' gasped the stout lawyer. 'I don't understand you.'

'You're under arrest,' said the other

calmly, and he whistled for a passing taxi to stop.

He hustled his prisoner into the cab, and Mr. Hake sank limply back on the leather seat. 'This is an outrage!' he stammered feebly. 'You've no right to arrest me — no right at all.'

'You will be given ample opportunity to make any complaint that you feel necessary, at Cannon Row,' retorted Inspector Marker pleasantly. 'In the meantime I must warn you that anything you say may be used in evidence against you.'

'But — but what's the charge?' demanded the lawyer. 'I am entitled to know what the charge is?'

'Conspiracy and accessory to murder!' said the inspector laconically, and the fat face of Mr. Hake went grey.

★ ★ ★

The bearded man unbarred the door of his cottage and let Mr. Frank Lane out into the night.

'The day after to-morrow, no later,' he

said, and there was a note of warning in his voice.

The other nodded. His face had changed during that interview. His sallow complexion was a dirty white, and the lines that had appeared about his eyes and at the corners of his mouth made him look old and worn.

'All right,' he said shortly, and he made his way back to Maddox Court.

The side door was still as he had left it, and he slipped in, bolting and chaining it behind him. Creeping up to his bedroom, he switched on the light and undressing got into bed. But he did not sleep. Throughout the night he lay staring into the gloom of the room, restless and wakeful, for he had received a shock such as he had never had before in his life!

29

Arrest!

The morning was wet and windy. A fine
rain fell incessantly, driven at an acute
angle before the gusts, so that it lashed
the faces of the people hurrying along the
streaming pavements of Whitehall. It
brought a tinge of pink even to the pale
cheeks of Chief-Inspector Trimmer as he
turned into the big archway leading to
Scotland Yard, and crossing the courtyard
beyond, entered the grim building.

But despite the unpleasantness of the
morning he was smiling, or rather he had
contorted his face into the extraordinary
grimace which passed with him for a
smile. He grunted a good morning to the
man on duty at the door, and climbed the
stairs to his office. Removing his dripping
overcoat and hat, he sat down at his desk
and pulled the telephone towards him.

'Put me through to Inspector Druse,'

he said when the clerk at the private exchange answered, and after a brief pause: 'Is that you, Druse? Trimmer this end. Listen! I want six good men an' a fast car.'

'When?' asked the voice at the other end of the wire.

Mr. Trimmer raised his eyes to the big clock on the opposite wall. 'It's ten o'clock now,' he answered, frowning thoughtfully. 'Say at eleven, will that be all right?'

'Sure,' said Druse. 'You can have 'em in five minutes if you want 'em.'

'Eleven will do,' said the chief-inspector, 'and listen. See that arms are issued to them, will you?'

The man he was speaking to whistled softly. 'What's up?' he enquired. 'Big job?'

'Very big,' answered Mr. Trimmer. 'The Maddox case.'

He gave a few more instructions and hung up the receiver. Searching in his waistcoat pocket, he took out a packet of Woodbines. He stuck one of these between his lips, lit it, and then leaning down, he pulled open a drawer and took out a folder. Laying this before him, he opened it and began to read with close attention the typed sheets it contained. One was signed in the sprawling writing of Mr. Frank Rabson, and the other bore at the bottom of the last sheet the neater signature of Mr. Hake. He had almost reached the last page of the second statement when there was a tap on the door and a constable entered.

'The car and the men are waiting, sir,' he said.

The chief-inspector rose, thrust the folder back in the drawer and pulled on his still wet coat and hat. He left the office and going down the stairs, made his way out to the Embankment entrance where a long-bonneted speedy-looking car was waiting filled with plain-clothes men. There was just room for Mr. Trimmer, and in spite of his thinness it was a tight squeeze.

'You know where you have to go to?' he said, and the driver nodded. 'All right then, let her go.'

The powerful car shot away from the kerb.

Charles Stroude turned away from the telephone impatiently.

'What's the matter with the thing, Gilder?' he asked. 'I can't get any reply from the exchange.'

The grey-haired butler shook his head. 'I don't know, sir,' he answered. 'Something went wrong with it early last evening. I tried to 'phone through to the grocer, sir, for some supplies we were requiring, and I couldn't get any reply either.'

'It's most awkward,' grumbled the secretary. 'I shall have to write to the exchange at once and get them to send someone to see to it. I was expecting a call from Mr. Hake, too.'

He went into the dining-room and stood staring out of the window at the rain-soaked grounds.

'Filthy weather!' he muttered, and then he looked round as a step sounded behind him.

Mr. Frank Lane had come into the room and his face was ghastly. The sleepless night had left its mark. He looked ten years older than he had done on the previous evening.

'What was that you were saying about the telephone to Gilder just now?' he said.

Stroude told him.

'Then — er — we can't get any messages through?' said Mr. Lane in consternation, and licked his dry lips. 'That is — er — unfortunate.'

He drifted out of the room again without another word, and Stroude looked after him curiously. What had happened to put the man in such a state of nerves? he wondered. He found no answer to the question, for he was ignorant of the other's nocturnal meeting with the bearded man.

Mr. Lane wandered disconsolately about the house trying to rid himself of the unpleasant feeling that hung over him. Margaret was nowhere to be found. She had gone up to her own room almost directly after breakfast, and had remained there ever since. Eventually he settled himself down in the drawing-room, and

355

tried to fix his attention on the newspaper. He was still occupied with this rather futile attempt at thought distraction when he heard the swish of wheels on wet gravel and the squeak of brakes. Laying down his paper he went over to the window, and looked out, but it was impossible to see the drive from this point. While he was still peering into the drizzle outside Gilder entered.

'Major Hilling and Inspector Burnett have called, sir,' said the butler.

Mr. Lane's sallow face whitened. The moment he had been dreading had come.

'You're sure they want me?' he asked.

'Yes, sir,' replied the butler.

'All right,' he said in a slightly husky voice. 'I'll — I'll see them.'

He followed Gilder out into the hall and entered the study. The trim, military figure of the chief constable was standing in front of the fireplace. Inspector Burnett was by the window looking out into the garden.

'Er — good morning,' said Mr. Lane. 'You wish to see me?'

Major Hilling bowed. 'Are you Mr.

Frank Lane?' he asked and the other nodded. 'I'm afraid, Mr. Lane, I have come on rather unpleasant business,' the chief constable went on, shaking his head. 'Business that concerns the murder of your uncle, Sir James Maddox.'

'Yes?' Mr. Lane felt his throat go very dry. 'Yes?'

'I should be obliged if you would ask Miss Maddox and Mr. Stroude to be present before I go any further,' said the major.

'Certainly.' Mr. Lane stepped over to the bell and pressed it.

There followed an awkward silence broken by the arrival of Gilder.

'Will you find Mr. Stroude and your mistress, Gilder,' said Mr. Lane nervously, 'and ask them if they will come here. Mr. — er — Major Hilling would like to see them.'

The butler withdrew.

'Sit down, won't you?' Mr. Lane pushed forward a chair, but the chief constable declined with a shake of the head.

'I should prefer to stand, thank you,' he

said briefly, and again there was an awkward silence.

Then the door opened, and Margaret Maddox came in followed by Charles Stroude.

'Good morning, Miss Maddox,' said the major. 'I'm exceedingly sorry to trouble you, but I am afraid it is very necessary. We have found the murderer of Sir James.'

The girl gave a low cry. 'Found — the murderer?' she whispered, and her face was ashen.

'Yes, miss.' It was Burnett who spoke, briskly and alertly. With one stride he stepped forward and laid his hand on the guilty man's shoulder. 'Charles Stroude,' he said sternly, 'I arrest you for the murder of Sir James Maddox in this room on the night of November 14th, and on a further charge of having entered in a conspiracy to obtain money by fraud! I have to warn you — '

'You're mad!' snarled Stroude. 'What proof have you got?'

'Signed statements by your associates, Frank Rabson and Joshua Hake,' snapped the inspector, 'and if any further proof is needed I think this man can supply it.'

He looked towards the door, and Stroude swung round, facing with glaring eyes the figure of the bearded man who had just been brought in by two plain-clothes detectives.

'So you've squealed, have you!' he cried. 'I'll settle you, you — '

He wrenched himself free from Burnett's grip and took a step forward, but from behind the little group at the door appeared the lank figure of Chief Inspector Trimmer, an automatic gripped in his lean hand.

'I don't think I should try that,' he said gently. 'Really I don't.'

'It's no good, Stroude,' said the man called Hocket, but his voice was no longer the voice of the gardener. 'It won't help you. We know everything.'

Stroude stared at him with dropped jaw as though he had seen a ghost. 'Good God!' he cried incredulously. 'It's that damned reporter!'

'Thought I was dead, didn't you?' said Peter pleasantly. 'I'm sorry to disappoint you — and your wife!'

He swung round on the cowering figure of the white-faced girl.

'Arrest that woman!' said Mr. Trimmer curtly, nodding to the two plain-clothes men. 'Her name is Elizabeth Stroude, and the charge is accessory to murder. She is not an' never has been the daughter of Sir James Maddox. His real daughter is here!'

Betty Hardy came hesitantly into the room.

30

A Scoop for the *Megaphone*

The pretty face of the girl known as Margaret Maddox became distorted and ugly. The full red lips curled back from her even teeth in a snarl that showed the gums, and her blue eyes narrowed to slits. She tried to wrench herself free from the grasp of the plain-clothes man who had come up behind her and gripped her by the arm.

'You swine!' She leaned forward and almost spat the word at Peter, her smooth soft voice harsh and rasping with the rage that consumed her. 'You swine! How did you manage to get away — that night?'

'Easy!' answered the reporter with a grin. 'You see I was expecting something to happen, and although your pal Hocket did his best I was too quick for him. You really should have chosen someone who was a better shot! His first two bullets went wide, and then mine got him in his pistol wrist. It was all over then as far as he was concerned. My first idea was to hand him straight over to the police, and then it occurred to me to take his place. He was of similar build and rather like me, except for the amount of hair. I tied him up, gagged him, and made him march into the obscurity of the wood, and there I talked to him until he saw reason. I'm afraid I gave poor old Burnett rather a bad time, but I had to leave the car because I didn't know whether anybody would come after Hocket to see if he'd done his job. I got him, eventually, to Cannon Row, and my friend Mr. Trimmer thought my idea was a good one, and arranged for the *Megaphone* to publish a perfectly erroneous account of the finding of my body.'

'God Almighty!' The words came in a hoarse croak from Stroude's throat. 'Then it was you I came to see at the hut. You who — who — '

'It was,' broke in Peter. 'I went there as soon as they'd made me up at the Yard to look like Hocket.'

'And I gave you the knife to — to — '
There was a dazed look in the secretary's
eyes as though he could not believe the
evidence of his own senses.

'To kill Miss Hardy?' Peter nodded.
'Yes, it was most useful! I used it to cut
her bonds and took her back to the hut
from which she was fetched by Burnett.
Since then she has been staying at
Burnett's house, looked after by his sister.
Of course, she told me how Hake had
kidnapped her, and brought her to
Maddox Court. She was hidden here in a
priest hole, the entrance of which is by a
panel over there.' He turned his head
towards one side of the room.

'Good Heavens, I know that place!'
muttered Mr. Lane. 'Everybody knew
about it. I thought it was screwed up.'

'It probably was until a day or so ago,'
said Peter.

'I wish Charlie had got you when he
fired at you through the window!' said the
girl through her clenched teeth.

'So it was Charlie who did that?' asked
Peter. 'I rather thought it might have
been, when I remembered later that the

drawing-room windows opened onto the same stretch of path as those to the study. But of course, at that time you provided him with a perfect alibi. I didn't know then that you were responsible for all this business.'

There was a pause, a complete and utter silence, and then quite suddenly the girl who had been known as Margaret Maddox laughed. It was a high-pitched mirthless sound, nervy and jarring.

'I'm glad you got that old fool Hake,' she cried surprisingly, 'and Rabson too. Bloody fools, both of them. Well, I suppose it's all over.'

'I'm afraid it is,' said the chief inspector mournfully, and Burnett laid his hand on the girl's shoulder.

'Elizabeth Stroude alias Margaret Maddox,' he said in his metallic official voice, 'I arrest you for having conspired to murder Sir James Maddox, William Sneath and Mrs. Berman. There will be other charges, and I must warn you — '

'Oh cut all that damned rot!' she broke in hysterically, and with a quick movement her hand went to her mouth.

'Stop her!' shouted Peter. He sprang forward, gripping at her wrist, but he was too late. The large pearl that she had worn in her ring was gone, the thin glass that it had been composed of crushed between those little white even teeth.

'You — can't — be — clever — all — the — time,' she whispered huskily, and he smelt the faint odour of bitter almonds. 'I was always prepared — in case of accid — '

She slid forward, and then collapsed to the floor. For a second her face twisted in pain, and then the muscles relaxed, and she seemed to be sleeping . . .

★ ★ ★

The *Megaphone* was the only newspaper that carried the full story, and even the taciturn Mr. Stevens was pleased. In an article under the heading of 'The Maddox Conspiracy, by Peter Escott,' the last veil was torn from the mystery surrounding the murder of Sir James.

' . . . It remains for me,' Peter wrote, 'to reveal the causes which led up to the tragic death of Sir James Maddox, the murder of William Sneath and the murder of the woman Annie Berman. Betty Stroude was the illegitimate daughter of Henry Skiller, the man who was hanged some years ago for the murder of an unfortunate grocer in Croydon. Mrs. Berman's sister, Sarah Rabson, was the mistress of this man, Skiller, but she left him owing to his cruel treatment six months before he was arrested, and went to live with her brother, Frank Rabson, who was nearly as bad a crook as Skiller himself. Seven months after she went to live with her brother and his wife at Rose Water Lane, Battersea, she gave birth to a child, a girl. At this time her sister, Mrs. Annie Berman, was nursing Sir James Maddox's wife, who had also given birth to a girl while her husband was in India. The two children were, as a matter of fact, born within a few days of each other. Sir James was sent for at once, but before he had time to reach England his wife died. The whole family of the Rabsons were crooks more or less, and it was Mrs. Berman who suggested that the babies should be changed before Sir James arrived home. Her brother was against this at first, but when she pointed out that it might enable them later on to blackmail Sir James and extract money from him, he agreed. Her original idea was that one of them should inform Sir James when the child had grown up, that she was not his real daughter, and demand a substantial sum for disclosing where his real daughter was to be found.

The babies were changed, but when Betty Skiller grew up, and attained an age when she could think for herself, she altered the original plan completely. Mrs. Berman had by this time been pensioned off by Sir James, but while she had acted as Betty's nurse, she had learned sufficient of the girl's character to realise that not only would she be an asset in any schemes they might have for getting money out of Sir James Maddox, but that she was far cleverer than they, and would probably be able to improve upon the original idea. So when she was old enough, she told her the whole story.

Betty Skiller, who was, of course,

known as Margaret Maddox, did improve upon the original scheme. She had tasted luxury, and she wasn't going to be thrown out of the comfortable life she was leading for the sake of a share in a few thousand pounds. She proposed a better plan.

Sir James, who was passionately fond of her, had already told her that at his death his money would come to her, and she suggested that they should wait for a year or two, and that then he should be got rid of, which would leave her in sole possession of his property. The others were rather horrified at first at this suggestion, but she talked them over. She was the prime mover in the business all the way through. It was her brain that planned everything. She had apparently inherited all the bad qualities of her father.

It was, however, useless killing Sir James until she was nearly twenty-one, because the will provided that the money should not come to her until she became of age.

During her stay at a finishing school in Paris, she came in contact, and fell in love, with a gentleman adventurer of the name of Stroude. He was a thorough bad lot, utterly unscrupulous, and before she came back to England they were secretly married. She took him into her confidence, and told him the whole plot, and he suggested that she should arrange with Sir James to engage him for a secretary.

In the meantime, the other girl whom they called Betty Hardy, was being looked after by Rabson's wife. There is no doubt that they treated her very badly, and that she was little more than a drudge. When she grew up they decided that she ought to have a job of some sort, and Stroude, who had discovered that Hake had been robbing Sir James for some years, and had the lawyer completely under his thumb, suggested that he should be made to take her as his secretary. In order to prepare herself for this, she was sent to a night school, and later entered the solicitor's establishment. Hake had to obey, as he had to obey all their other orders, for they held the fear of exposure and consequent long term of imprisonment over him.

The time now drew near for the final act of the drama, but it had to be anticipated by nearly three months owing to a totally unforeseen development. William Sneath, a blackmailer and police informer, who was afterwards murdered, and who also lived in Rose Water Lane, got curious about Rabson and the visitor he received so often in a closed car. By some means or other he discovered the whole scheme and saw in it a chance of making money for himself.

He telephoned to Sir James, asking for an appointment, and without actually stating his business said enough to arouse Sir James's suspicions. Very naturally, Sir James consulted Hake, and the solicitor, having pooh-poohed the whole thing, advised him not to take any notice of it, and immediately notified Stroude.

In the meantime the girl masquerading as Margaret Maddox received a letter from Sneath demanding a large sum to keep his mouth shut under the threat of divulging his knowledge to Sir James. Sneath's idea was apparently to play one off against the other, and see which would reap him the biggest reward. Betty Stroude talked things over with her husband, and they came to the conclusion that the time was ripe for the removal of the old man. Sneath might at any minute give the whole plot away to Sir James, and so there was reason for haste.

I have already outlined the plot they hatched for carrying out the murder at the beginning of this article. It was Hake who suggested that Dick Mason should be the victim. He had heard about his circumstances from Betty Hardy, and concluded that he was ideal for the purpose.

Rabson was the man who met him and persuaded him to take the letter. Just before Mason was timed to arrive at Maddox Court, Stroude entered the study on the pretext of asking Sir James a question concerning some work he was doing for him, killed him, wiped the poker clean, and concealing himself behind the curtains waited for Mason to arrive. When he arrived Stroude knocked him out, and took away the letter so that there should be no evidence to confirm his improbable story.

Unfortunately for Stroude, William Sneath saw the crime committed. Getting no satisfaction from Betty Stroude, and no answer to a letter he had written to Sir James, again asking for an appointment, he came down to Maddox Court with the determination of seeing one or other of them, and settling the business one way or the other. He arrived a few minutes before Mason, concealing himself in some bushes near the french windows when he heard him approaching along the path leading from the drive.

His witnessing of the crime gave him a greater hold than before. He rang up Stroude, threatening to go straight to the police unless he was paid the sum of twenty thousand pounds by return. Stroude agreed to his demands and suggested a meeting place. Rabson was notified and got hold of a taxi from a garage in Southampton Row, and arrived, with Stroude inside, at the meeting place which was opposite Battersea Town Hall.

Sneath was waiting, and Stroude told

him that Betty Stroude wished to see him herself, and persuaded him to get inside the cab. As soon as they had left London and reached a lonely part of the country Stroude shot him. Rabson drove the cab on, leaving Stroude within a few miles of Maddox Court. Near Putney he abandoned the taxi after leaving Sneath's body at the side of the road, and returned to Battersea by train.

When I arrived at Maddox Court with Inspector Burnett to make my first enquiries into the murder, Stroude had just returned from the killing of William Sneath. They thought that after this everything would be plain sailing, but Mrs. Berman began to get difficult. She wanted more than had been agreed upon. When she turned up at Hake's office the day I was there and nearly gave the whole thing away in her drunken rage, she signed her own death warrant. Stroude went down to Horsham and killed her.

I have been able to tell this story in such detail because of the statements made by Rabson, Hake and the man Hocket which are now in the possession of the police. It is a sordid story, and the end will be written when Charles Stroude, and his three accomplices pay the penalty for their crimes . . . '

★   ★   ★

It was a very resplendent Peter who one morning some months later met the lugubrious Mr. Trimmer in the Strand. The chief inspector stopped and eyed him disparagingly.

'What's the idea of the glad rags?' he asked, pointing to the reporter's immaculate morning suit.

Peter grinned. 'Just been to a wedding,' he announced.

Mr. Trimmer grunted. 'Thought you'd got something better to do than waste your time,' he said gloomily. 'Who's bin married?'

'You know them,' answered Peter. 'Margaret Maddox and Dick Mason.'

The chief inspector shook his head sadly.

'I thought that was goin' to happen,' he said. 'We saved him from bein' hanged, an' now he's gone and got himself sentenced for life. I should have thought the poor chap had been through enough!'

THE END

Books by Gerald Verner
in the Linford Mystery Library:

THE LAST WARNING
DENE OF THE SECRET SERVICE
THE NURSERY RHYME MURDERS
TERROR TOWER
THE CLEVERNESS OF MR. BUDD
THE SEVEN LAMPS
THEY WALK IN DARKNESS
THE HEEL OF ACHILLES
DEAD SECRET
MR. BUDD STEPS IN
THE RETURN OF MR. BUDD
MR. BUDD AGAIN
QUEER FACE
THE CRIMSON RAMBLERS
GHOST HOUSE
THE ANGEL
DEATH SET IN DIAMONDS
THE CLUE OF THE GREEN CANDLE
THE 'Q' SQUAD
MR. BUDD INVESTIGATES
THE RIVER HOUSE MYSTERY
NOOSE FOR A LADY

THE FACELESS ONES
GRIM DEATH
MURDER IN MANUSCRIPT
THE GLASS ARROW
THE THIRD KEY
THE ROYAL FLUSH MURDERS

We do hope that you have enjoyed reading this large print book.

Did you know that all of our titles are available for purchase?

We publish a wide range of high quality large print books including:
Romances, Mysteries, Classics
General Fiction
Non Fiction and Westerns

Special interest titles available in large print are:
The Little Oxford Dictionary
Music Book, Song Book
Hymn Book, Service Book

Also available from us courtesy of Oxford University Press:
Young Readers' Dictionary
(large print edition)
Young Readers' Thesaurus
(large print edition)

For further information or a free brochure, please contact us at:
Ulverscroft Large Print Books Ltd.,
The Green, Bradgate Road, Anstey,
Leicester, LE7 7FU, England.
Tel: (00 44) 0116 236 4325
Fax: (00 44) 0116 234 0205

Other titles in the
Linford Mystery Library:

THE FILE ON
COLONEL MORAN

Vernon Mealor

An exciting trio of tales following the escapades of Colonel Sebastian Moran, 'one of the best shots in the world' and the 'second most dangerous man in London', according to Sherlock Holmes. Find out how Moran achieves his position at the right hand of Professor Moriarty in 'The Hurlstone Selection'; shares lodgings with Holmes, Watson, and Mrs Hudson in 'The Man with the Square-Toed Boots'; and turns his skills to art theft in 'The Disappearance of Lord Lexingham'.

THE THIRD KEY

Gerald Verner

The Reverend Colin Armitage receives a parcel one morning containing a key and the intriguing message: 'This is Bluebeard's first key.' The key belongs to the cottage of a woman named Sylvia Shand, who is found there, strangled. A few days later, Bluebeard's second key arrives by post and the district nurse is found strangled in similar circumstances. The police believe a homicidal maniac is loose in the village but Armitage has other ideas. And then a third key arrives . . .

MORE CASES OF A PRIVATE EYE

Ernest Dudley

This second book of Ernest Dudley's stories about his London-based private eye character, Nat Craig, finds Craig's clients making up a pretty varied collection. Young, wealthy women getting themselves blackmailed; wealthier men or women who have the jitters over the safety of their precious family heirlooms; occasionally even members of the ex-crook class, appeal to him for help. And not infrequently Craig finds himself confronted with grisly murders, testing his tough resourcefulness and considerable powers of deduction.

A CANDIDATE FOR CONSPIRACY

Steve Hayes

Yesterday he was a spy. Today he's a Washington politician. Tomorrow he could be the next President of the United States. Soon he could be in control of one of the world's most powerful nations — unless a daredevil adventurer and his beautiful accomplice can stop him. But that's a big if . . .